CW01237431

White Teeth, Red Blood

Selected Vampiric Verses

CLAIRE KOHDA's debut novel, *Woman, Eating*, was a *New Yorker* book of the year. Her essays, short fiction and reviews have appeared in the *Guardian*, *TLS*, *Financial Times* and *New York Times*, among other outlets.

White Teeth, Red Blood

Selected Vampiric Verses
With an Introduction by Claire Kohda

Pushkin Press

Pushkin Press
Somerset House, Strand
London WC2R 1LA

Introduction © Claire Kohda 2025

Selection and arrangement © Pushkin Press 2025

First published by Pushkin Press in 2025

ISBN 13: 978-1-80533-264-0

Translation of "Metamorphoses of the Vampire" by Charles Baudelaire from *Flowers of Evil* © George Dillon and Edna St Vincent Millay 1936, renewed © 1963 by George Dillon and Norma Millay Ellis. Reprinted with the permission of the Edna St Vincent Millay Society. Every effort has been made to contact the owner of George Dillon's copyright. If you are the owner please contact Pushkin Press.

"I Am a Cowboy in the Boat of Ra" from *New and Collected Poems* © Ishmael Reed 1988, 2000 and 2006. Reprinted with the permission of Lowenstein Associates.

"The Distant Moon" from *The Other Man Was Me* © Rafael Campo 1994. Reprinted with the permission of Arte Público Press.

"Pocket Vampire" from *American Fanatics* © Dorothy Barresi 2010. Reprinted with the permission of the University of Pittsburgh Press.

"Charles Baudelaire and I Meet in the Oval Garden"
© John Yau 2022. Reprinted with the permission of the author.

Translation of "The Vampire" by Delmira Agustini © Tim and Sofia Smith-Laing 2025. Reprinted with the permission of the translators.

All rights reserved. No part of this publication may be reproduced, stored in a retrieval system or transmitted in any form or by any means, electronic, mechanical, photocopying, recording or otherwise, without prior permission in writing from Pushkin Press

A CIP catalogue record for this title is available from the British Library

The authorised representative in the EEA is
eucomply OÜ, Pärnu mnt. 139b-14, 11317, Tallinn, Estonia,
hello@eucompliancepartner.com, +33757690241

Designed and typeset in Spectrum by Tetragon, London
Printed and bound in the United Kingdom by Clays Ltd, Elcograf S.p.A.

Pushkin Press is committed to a sustainable future for our business, our readers and our planet. This book is made from paper from forests that support responsible forestry.

www.pushkinpress.com

1 3 5 7 9 8 6 4 2

CONTENTS

Introduction by Claire Kohda   9

CHILLING TALES

GOTTFRIED AUGUST BURGER
Lenore   19

JOHANN WOLFGANG VON GOETHE
The Bride of Corinth   29

ROBERT SOUTHEY
From *Thalaba the Destroyer*   39

ANNE BANNERMAN
The Dark Ladie   62

JOHN STAGG
The Vampyre   69

LORD BYRON
From *The Giaour*   75

SAMUEL TAYLOR COLERIDGE
Christabel   113

ALFRED, LORD TENNYSON
From *Maud*   138

RAFAEL CAMPO
The Distant Moon   158

DIRE WARNINGS

HEINRICH AUGUST OSSENFELDER
The Vampire — 163

JOHN KEATS
La Belle Dame Sans Merci — 164

HENRY THOMAS LIDDELL
The Vampire Bride — 166

JAMES CLERK MAXWELL
The Vampyre — 167

CHARLES BAUDELAIRE
Metamorphoses of the Vampire — 170

CHRISTINA ROSSETTI
A Daughter of Eve — 172

MADISON JULIUS CAWEIN
The Vampire — 173

RUDYARD KIPLING
The Vampire — 175

CONRAD AIKEN
The Vampire — 177

EDNA ST VINCENT MILLAY
Witch-Wife — 181

JAMES WELDON JOHNSON
The White Witch — 182

THE VAMPIRE WITHIN

ANNA LÆTITIA BARBAULD
*To a Little Invisible Being Who is Expected
Soon to Become Visible* ... 187

EMILY BRONTË
Ah! Why, Because the Dazzling Sun ... 189

EMILY DICKINSON
A Death blow is a Life blow to Some (816) ... 191

WALTER PATER
The Mona Lisa Paragraph from The Renaissance ... 192

DELMIRA AGUSTINI
The Vampire ... 194

WILLIAM BUTLER YEATS
Oil and Blood ... 195

ISHMAEL REED
I Am a Cowboy in the Boat of Ra ... 196

DOROTHY BARRESI
Pocket Vampire ... 199

JOHN YAU
Charles Baudelaire and I Meet in the Oval Garden ... 200

INTRODUCTION

When I was asked to introduce this book, I thought that I was perhaps the worst person to do so. I didn't grow up reading vampire fiction, or horror, and I wouldn't consider myself a vampire fan, even though I have written a novel whose main character is a vampire.

I think, however, that very few of the authors represented in these pages wrote about vampires because they were vampire fans. Byron likely wasn't obsessed with vampires (though one of the earliest literary vampires is based on him). Neither was Emily Dickinson, and probably neither was Kipling (though he, of everyone included in this book, is to my mind the most likely to have actually been a vampire; at least, with the colonialist, exoticizing and fetishizing under(over)tones of his work, he is one of the most vampiric). All the writers in this book, rather, were drawn to the vampire as a metaphor or device.

The vampire, for a writer, is an alluring figure. It straddles life and death, is often nocturnal, or at least inhabits shadows or the dark, and must drain living things of blood in order to survive. It is a creature that looks like us humans but has a different diet; it is a slightly different species, but one that can exist amongst humans undetected. In essence, it is different, other. Loneliness, alienation, morality, mortality, humanity, inhumanity: all can be explored through the vampire, plus any form of difference: neurodivergence, foreignness, disability, illness, gender and sexuality, for instance. Vampires are also full of contradictions. Alive, but dead; often beautiful, but abhorrent; sometimes sexy, despite having been dead for centuries; self-flagellating and hungry; powerful, superhuman, yet sometimes vulnerable and fragile. Very old vampires are anachronisms: they are living history, bringing the past right into the present, with all the traumas of the past. Every one of us who has written about a vampire knows our own vampire very well, because each reflects something of what we thought of humanity at the time we wrote them. But perhaps none of us could do justice to introducing this book.

A vampire is defined differently depending on who you speak to. Many cultures have blood-sucking creatures in their mythologies. The Balinese *léyak*, for instance, appears human during the day, but after dark, its head and internal organs break away from their body and fly through the night looking for newborn babies to drain of blood. The *langsuyar* of Malaysia is a woman who becomes a flying vampire-like creature after the stillbirth of her child; while the *pontianak* is a woman who has died during childbirth and feasts on the blood of men. The *sasabonsam* of Ghana hangs upside down from trees like a bat, then swoops down and eats its victims, thumbs first. Then there is the *yara-ma-yha-who*, a creature from Australian Aboriginal folklore that resembles a small frog-like man who drains its victims' blood using suckers on its hands and feet. The vampire in this collection is the Western vampire: the bloodsucker who bites victims' necks, drains blood to survive, is human in appearance, immortal, and whose lineage includes figures such as Dracula and Nosferatu.

However, all these creatures are related. Often colonialism creates new vampires, such as the *soucouyant* of the Caribbean; myths from different cultures combine to create new monsters; and often their bloodsucking stands for the real-life draining of a country's and a people's culture and resources. Vampire-like myths have also travelled back to the West and come to represent in the Western mind fear of the other, of difference, immigration, the foreigner, and of revenge by colonial and/or enslaved subjects. Bloodsuckers are in this way often cousins.

You can read this collection in any order. However, it is divided into three sections. "Chilling Tales" contains unsettling poems that you can imagine reading by candlelight, including many long narrative poems from the eighteenth and nineteenth centuries, an under-read and overlooked form. "Dire Warnings" sees the wrath of a vampire often imagined as punishment for war-mongering, sexual promiscuity, or for a woman rejecting a man, the latter in Heinrich August Ossenfelder's violent poem *The Vampire* from 1748, in which the male protagonist imagines himself as a vampire sneaking into a woman's room after she has rejected him, and taking "her life's blood". In "The Vampire Within", the vampire is less definable. In the often more interior and insular poems here, it acts as a metaphor for many things, from pregnancy and art to racism and colonialism.

These sections are chronological, charting the evolution of the Western vampire from its early origins to its most recent incarnations. I began at the end and worked backwards, starting with the vampire closest to my own, in time and in origin—a 2022 vampire in Chinese-American poet, art critic and curator John Yau's *Charles Baudelaire and I Meet in the Oval Garden*. The dual identities of the vampire intrigue me: dead/alive, inhuman/human, other/familiar; and Yau's writing often explores the dualities of East and West, of visual art and writing. Here, Yau writes a Malaysian verse form called a pantoum, popular with nineteenth-century French poets, in which the second and fourth lines become the first and third lines in the next stanza, giving the poem a woven quality. One line reads: "They say that the latest strain hiding in the shadows is a yellow vampire"—an allusion, perhaps, to the Covid-19 pandemic during which people of Asian descent were subjected to hate and blamed for the virus; the monstrousness of the vampire represents the virus itself and the dehumanization of Asians at the time. Further back, in Ishmael Reed's singingly musical 1972 poem, *I Am a Cowboy in the Boat of Ra*, the vampire is Set (god of, among much else, violence and foreigners), and he symbolizes the suppression of native religions by foreign powers, an "imposter" and "usurper", a "party pooper O hater of dance". The protagonist goes out after him, "to unseat Set", "to Set down Set". Neither Reed's nor Yau's poem is of the horror genre;

but the inclusion of the vampire highlights the horrors of humanity.

Walter Pater's famous description of the *Mona Lisa* isn't strictly a poem but rather a paragraph lifted from his essay on Leonardo da Vinci in his 1873 book *The Renaissance: Studies in Art and Poetry*; though W.B. Yeats described it as "the first modern poem" and published a sentence from it (beginning "She is older than…"), broken up into lines to more closely resemble poetry, in *The Oxford Book of Modern Verse* in 1936. In this original version, the Mona Lisa is a "vampire": timeless, immortal, containing "all the thoughts and experience of the world… the animalism of Greece, the lust of Rome…", "older than the rocks among which she sits". The Mona Lisa as vampire is a comment on art, not just this portrait—but the mysterious vitality at the centre of all works of art that, as if by magic, connect us to and preserve the past, while continuing to comment on the present.

The boundaries between life and death (and life again) are blurry for vampires. Emily Dickinson's 1866 poem *A Death blow is a Life blow to Some* can read on the surface like a vampire poem where the life–death boundary is blurred, but also uses the idea of returning to life after a "death blow" to deliver a message: don't wait until death comes to truly start living. Anna Lætitia Barbauld's *To a Little Invisible Being* focuses on the divide between life and death too, but addresses an unborn child, still in the womb, waiting to arrive: "Haste," she writes, "through life's mysterious gate". And then, in American poet and physician Rafael Campo's 1994 poem *The Distant Moon*, a doctor takes care of a dying patient; the vampire is only a brief metaphor in passing—the doctor drawing blood, "You'll make me live forever!" says the patient. "The darkened halls" here are not of a vampire's manor but of a hospital, but just as occupied by both life and death; "he was so near / Death" reads one line break which can be read in many ways: the patient physically close to the doctor, Death metaphorically close to the patient, the patient nearly gone and, so, in fact, getting more distant from the doctor.

The vampire is often a woman—a sinful temptress or witch – who preys on men. Conrad Aiken's *The Vampire*, written in 1914, characterizes war as a female vampire possessing "terrible beauty", perhaps also alluding to suffragettes, who at the time were seen as terrorists. The men in this poem give in to her, "with mouth so sweet, so poisonous", until the ground is strewn with bodies and a ploughman is driving "through flesh and bone". In Madison Julius Cawein's 1896 poem, the speaker is seduced, then bound by "witch-words… to a fiend / Until I die". But go back to 1816, and in the section "Chilling Tales" is one of several long story-poems in this collection: the eerie, gothic, unfinished ballad *Christabel* by Samuel Taylor Coleridge. Here the vampiric figure Geraldine is a woman, as is Christabel, her victim. This is a sexually suggestive poem; Christabel falls under Geraldine's spell, undresses and lies down with her. In Coleridge's time, this would have been read as Christabel having been tempted into – or compelled into – sin, into lesbianism. However, Geraldine is a complex vampiric figure. She comes across as a temptation rather than a straightforward threat, and her encounter with Christabel is secretive, but not unpleasant. When Geraldine undresses, it reads, "Behold! her bosom and half her side — / A sight to dream of, not to tell!" Contrasting with Ossenfelder's *The Vampire*, in which a man fantasizes about draining his victim's "life's blood" and vampirism very explicitly suggests sexual violence, Geraldine is depicted holding Christabel: "in her arms the maid she took".*

The earliest ghoul (not quite vampire) in this collection is male. Gottfried August Burger's 1774 poem *Lenore* — together with Johann Wolfgang von Goethe's 1797 poem *The Bride of Corinth* — was an inspiration for a lot of early vampire literature, including Bram Stoker's *Dracula* (which quotes the line "the dead travel fast" or "die Todten reiten schnell", translated here by Dante Rossetti as "the dead gallop fast"). In *Lenore,* a soldier called William returns from the dead to his grieving wife and whisks her off on horseback to a cemetery where his human visage falls away, revealing that, underneath, he is Death, "fleshless and hairless... The lifelike mask was there no more". The Earth itself responds: "Groans from the earth and shrieks in the air! Howling and wailing everywhere!" Many consider this poem the origin of Western

---

* Lord Byron read *Christabel* aloud to his guests in a house on Lake Geneva in 1816. Percy Shelley, one of the guests, had to leave the room after a couple of lines and be treated by a doctor. From that came the idea for everyone present to write a scary story. John William Polidori wrote an influential short story called *The Vampyre*, basing his vampire on Byron; Byron wrote several poems, and Mary Wollstonecraft Godwin (later Mary Shelley) wrote *Frankenstein*, considered by many the first science fiction novel.

vampire literature – yet there is no bloodsucking, there are no fangs; just grief, horror and the sense of something deeply wrong. The vampire endures as a literary device because this is what is at its heart; it is a creature that evokes the most horrifying and often difficult aspects of human life. In the opposites that exist so close to the surface in a vampire – terror, violence, repulsion and monstrousness, alongside love, romance, attraction and beauty – are reflected something of the incomprehensibility of our world.

CLAIRE KOHDA

Chilling Tales

Lenore

GOTTFRIED AUGUST BURGER 1774

Translated by Dante Gabriel Rossetti

Up rose Lenore as the red morn wore,
    From weary visions starting;
"Art faithless, William, or, William, art dead?
    'Tis long since thy departing."
For he, with Frederick's men of might,
In fair Prague waged the uncertain fight;
Nor once had he writ in the hurry of war,
And sad was the true heart that sickened afar.

The Empress and the King,
    With ceaseless quarrel tired,
At length relaxed the stubborn hate
    Which rivalry inspired:
And the martial throng, with laugh and song,
Spoke of their homes as they rode along,
And clank, clank, clank! came every rank,
With the trumpet-sound that rose and sank.

And here and there and everywhere,
    Along the swarming ways,
Went old man and boy, with the music of joy,
    On the gallant bands to gaze;

And the young child shouted to spy the vaward,
And trembling and blushing the bride pressed forward:
But ah! for the sweet lips of Lenore
The kiss and the greeting are vanished and o'er.

From man to man all wildly she ran
    With a swift and searching eye;
But she felt alone in the mighty mass,
    As it crushed and crowded by:
On hurried the troop,—a gladsome group,—
And proudly the tall plumes wave and droop:
She tore her hair and she turned her round,
And madly she dashed her against the ground.

Her mother clasped her tenderly,
    With soothing words and mild:
"My child, may God look down on thee,—
    God comfort thee, my child."
"Oh! mother, mother! gone is gone!
I reck no more how the world runs on:
What pity to me does God impart?
Woe, woe, woe! for my heavy heart!"

"Help, Heaven, help and favour her!
    Child, utter an Ave Marie!
Wise and great are the doings of God;
    He loves and pities thee."
"Out, mother, out, on the empty lie!
Doth he heed my despair,—doth he list to my cry?
What boots it now to hope or to pray?
The night is come,—there is no more day."

"Help, Heaven, help! who knows the Father
    Knows surely that he loves his child:
The bread and the wine from the hand divine
    Shall make thy tempered grief less wild."
"Oh! mother, dear mother! the wine and the bread
Will not soften the anguish that bows down my head;
For bread and for wine it will yet be as late
That his cold corpse creeps from the grim grave's gate."

"What if the traitor's false faith failed,
    By sweet temptation tried,—
What if in distant Hungary
    He clasp another bride?—
Despise the fickle fool, my girl,
Who hath ta'en the pebble and spurned the pearl:
While soul and body shall hold together
In his perjured heart shall be stormy weather."

"Oh! mother, mother! gone is gone,
    And lost will still be lost!
Death, death is the goal of my weary soul,
    Crushed and broken and crost.
Spark of my life! down, down to the tomb:
Die away in the night, die away in the gloom!
What pity to me does God impart?
Woe, woe, woe! for my heavy heart!"

"Help, Heaven, help, and heed her not,
    For her sorrows are strong within;
She knows not the words that her tongue repeats,—
    Oh! count them not for sin!

Cease, cease, my child, thy wretchedness,
And think on the promised happiness;
So shall thy mind's calm ecstasy
Be a hope and a home and a bridegroom to thee."

"My mother, what is happiness?
   My mother, what is Hell?
With William is my happiness,—
   Without him is my Hell!
Spark of my life! down, down to the tomb:
Die away in the night, die away in the gloom!
Earth and Heaven, and Heaven and earth,
Reft of William are nothing worth."

Thus grief racked and tore the breast of Lenore,
   And was busy at her brain;
Thus rose her cry to the Power on high,
   To question and arraign:
Wringing her hands and beating her breast,—
Tossing and rocking without any rest;—
Till from her light veil the moon shone thro',
And the stars leapt out on the darkling blue.

But hark to the clatter and the pat pat patter!
   Of a horse's heavy hoof!
How the steel clanks and rings as the rider springs!
   How the echo shouts aloof!
While slightly and lightly the gentle bell
Tingles and jingles softly and well;
And low and clear through the door plank thin
Comes the voice without to the ear within:

"Holla! holla! unlock the gate;
    Art waking, my bride, or sleeping?
Is thy heart still free and still faithful to me?
    Art laughing, my bride, or weeping?"
"Oh! wearily, William, I've waited for you,—
Woefully watching the long day thro',—
With a great sorrow sorrowing
For the cruelty of your tarrying."

"Till the dead midnight we saddled not,—
    I have journeyed far and fast—
And hither I come to carry thee back
    Ere the darkness shall be past."
"Ah! rest thee within till the night's more calm;
Smooth shall thy couch be, and soft, and warm:
Hark to the winds, how they whistle and rush
Thro' the twisted twine of the hawthorn-bush."

"Thro' the hawthorn-bush let whistle and rush,—
    Let whistle, child, let whistle!
Mark the flash fierce and high of my steed's bright eye,
    And his proud crest's eager bristle.
Up, up and away! I must not stay:
Mount swiftly behind me! up, up and away!
An hundred miles must be ridden and sped
Ere we may lie down in the bridal-bed."

"What! ride an hundred miles to-night,
    By thy mad fancies driven!
Dost hear the bell with its sullen swell,
    As it rumbles out eleven?"

"Look forth! look forth! the moon shines bright:
We and the dead gallop fast thro' the night.
'Tis for a wager I bear thee away
To the nuptial couch ere break of day."

"Ah! where is the chamber, William dear,
    And William, where is the bed?"
"Far, far from here: still, narrow, and cool;
    Plank and bottom and lid."
"Hast room for me?"—"For me and thee;
Up, up to the saddle right speedily!
The wedding-guests are gathered and met,
And the door of the chamber is open set."

She busked her well, and into the selle
    She sprang with nimble haste,—
And gently smiling, with a sweet beguiling,
    Her white hands clasped his waist:—
And hurry, hurry! ring, ring, ring!
To and fro they sway and swing;
Snorting and snuffing they skim the ground,
And the sparks spurt up, and the stones run round.

Here to the right and there to the left
    Flew fields of corn and clover,
And the bridges flashed by to the dazzled eye,
    As rattling they thundered over.
"What ails my love? the moon shines bright:
Bravely the dead men ride through the night.
Is my love afraid of the quiet dead?"
"Ah! no;— let them sleep in their dusty bed!"

On the breeze cool and soft what tune floats aloft,
    While the crows wheel overhead?—
Ding dong! ding dong! 'tis the sound, 'tis the song,—
    "Room, room for the passing dead!"
Slowly the funeral-train drew near.
Bearing the coffin, bearing the bier;
And the chime of their chaunt was hissing and harsh,
Like the note of the bull-frog within the marsh.

"You bury your corpse at the dark midnight,
    With hymns and bells and wailing;—
But I bring home my youthful wife
    To a bride-feast's rich regaling.
Come, chorister, come with thy choral throng,
And solemnly sing me a marriage-song;
Come, friar, come,—let the blessing be spoken,
That the bride and the bridegroom's sweet rest be unbroken."

Died the dirge and vanished the bier:—
    Obedient to his call,
Hard hard behind, with a rush like the wind,
    Came the long steps' pattering fall:
And ever further! ring, ring, ring!
To and fro they sway and swing;
Snorting and snuffing they skim the ground,
And the sparks spurt up, and the stones run round.

How flew to the right, how flew to the left,
    Trees, mountains in the race!
How to the left, and the right and the left,
    Flew town and market-place!

"What ails my love? the moon shines bright:
Bravely the dead men ride thro' the night.
Is my love afraid of the quiet dead?"
"Ah! let them alone in their dusty bed!"

See, see, see! by the gallows-tree,
    As they dance on the wheel's broad hoop,
Up and down, in the gleam of the moon
    Half lost, an airy group:—
"Ho! ho! mad mob, come hither amain,
And join in the wake of my rushing train;—
Come, dance me a dance, ye dancers thin.
Ere the planks of the marriage-bed close us in."

And hush, hush, hush! the dreamy rout
    Came close with a ghastly bustle,
Like the whirlwind in the hazel-bush,
    When it makes the dry leaves rustle:
And faster, faster! ring, ring, ring!
To and fro they sway and swing;
Snorting and snuffing they skim the ground,
And the sparks spurt up, and the stones run round.

How flew the moon high overhead,
    In the wild race madly driven!
In and out, how the stars danced about.
    And reeled o'er the flashing heaven!
"What ails my love? the moon shines bright:
Bravely the dead men ride thro' the night.
Is my love afraid of the quiet dead?"
"Alas! let them sleep in their dusty bed."

"Horse, horse! meseems 'tis the cock's shrill note,
    And the sand is well nigh spent;
Horse, horse, away! 'tis the break of day,—
    'Tis the morning air's sweet scent.
Finished, finished is our ride:
Room, room for the bridegroom and the bride!
At last, at last, we have reached the spot,
For the speed of the dead man has slackened not!"

And swiftly up to an iron gate
    With reins relaxed they went;
At the rider's touch the bolts flew back,
    And the bars were broken and bent;
The doors were burst with a deafening knell,
And over the white graves they dashed pell mell;
The tombs around looked grassy and grim,
As they glimmered and glanced in the moonlight dim.

But see! but see! in an eyelid's beat,
    Towhoo! a ghastly wonder!
The horseman's jerkin, piece by piece,
    Dropped off like brittle tinder!
Fleshless and hairless, a naked skull,
The sight of his weird head was horrible;
The lifelike mask was there no more,
And a scythe and a sandglass the skeleton bore.

Loud snorted the horse as he plunged and reared,
    And the sparks were scattered round:—
What man shall say if he vanished away,
    Or sank in the gaping ground?

Groans from the earth and shrieks in the air!
Howling and wailing everywhere!
Half dead, half living, the soul of Lenore
Fought as it never had fought before.

The churchyard troop,—a ghostly group,—
    Close round the dying girl;
Out and in they hurry and spin
    Through the dance's weary whirl:
"Patience, patience, when the heart is breaking;
With thy God there is no question-making:
Of thy body thou art quit and free:
Heaven keep thy soul eternally!"

The Bride of Corinth

JOHANN WOLFGANG VON GOETHE   1797

Translated by William Edmondstoune Aytoun and Theodore Martin

I.

A youth to Corinth, whilst the city slumbered,
    Came from Athens: though a stranger there,
Soon among its townsmen to be numbered,
    For a bride awaits him, young and fair.
        From their childhood's years
        They were plighted feres,
    So contracted by their parents' care.

II.

But may not his welcome there he hindered?
    Dearly must he buy it, would he speed.
He is still a heathen with his kindred,
    She and hers washed in the Christian creed.
        When new faiths are born,
        Love and troth are torn
    Rudely from the heart, howe'er it bleed.

III.

All the house is hushed;—to rest retreated
    Father, daughters—not the mother quite;
She the guest with cordial welcome greeted,
    Led him to a room with tapers bright;
        Wine and food she brought,
        Ere of them he thought,
    Then departed with a fair good-night.

IV.

But he felt no hunger, and unheeded
    Left the wine, and eager for the rest
Which his limbs, forspent with travel, needed,
    On the couch he laid him, still undressed.
        There he sleeps—when lo!
        Onwards gliding slow,
    At the door appears a wondrous guest.

V.

By the waning lamp's uncertain gleaming
    There he sees a youthful maiden stand,
Robed in white, of still and gentle seeming,
    On her brow a black and golden band.
        When she meets his eyes,
        With a quick surprise
    Starting, she uplifts a pallid hand.

VI.

"Is a stranger here, and nothing told me?
    Am I then forgotten even in name?
Ah! 'tis thus within my cell they hold me,
    And I now am covered o'er with shame!
        Pillow still thy head
        There upon thy bed,
    I will leave thee quickly as I came."

VII.

"Maiden—darling! Stay, O stay!" and, leaping
    From the couch, before her stands the boy:
"Ceres—Bacchus, here their gifts are heaping,
    And thou bringest Amor's gentle joy!
        Why with terror pale?
        Sweet one, let us hail
    These bright gods—their festive gifts employ."

VIII.

"Oh, no—no! Young stranger, come not nigh me;
    Joy is not for me, nor festive cheer.
Ah! such bliss may ne'er be tasted by me,
    Since my mother, in fantastic fear,
        By long sickness bowed,
        To heaven's service vowed
    Me, and all the hopes that warmed me here.

IX.

"They have left our hearth, and left it lonely—
    The old gods, that bright and jocund train.
One, unseen, in heaven, is worshipped only.
    And upon the cross a Saviour slain;
        Sacrifice is here,
        Not of lamb nor steer,
    But of human woe and human pain."

X.

And he asks, and all her words doth ponder—
    "Can it be, that, in this silent spot,
I behold thee, thou surpassing wonder!
    My sweet bride, so strangely to me brought?
        Be mine only now—
        See, our parents' vow
    Heaven's good blessing hath for us besought."

XI.

"No! thou gentle heart," she cried in anguish;
    "'Tis not mine, but 'tis my sister's place;
When in lonely cell I weep and languish,
    Think, oh think of me in her embrace!
        I think but of thee—
        Pining drearily,
    Soon beneath the earth to hide my face!"

XII.

"Nay! I swear by yonder flame which burneth,
    Fanned by Hymen, lost thou shalt not be;
Droop not thus, for my sweet bride returneth
    To my father's mansion back with me!
        Dearest, tarry here!
        Taste the bridal cheer,
    For our spousal spread so wondrously!"

XIII.

Then with word and sign their troth they plighted,
    Golden was the chain she bade him wear,
But the cup he offered her she slighted,
    Silver, wrought with cunning past compare.
        "That is not for me;
        All I ask of thee
    Is one little ringlet of thy hair!"

XIV.

Dully boomed the midnight hour unhallowed,
    And then first her eyes began to shine;
Eagerly with pallid lips she swallowed
    Hasty draughts of purple-tinctured wine;
        But the wheaten bread,
        As in shuddering dread,
    Put she always by with loathing sign.

XV.

And she gave the youth the cup: he drained it,
   With impetuous haste he drained it dry;
Love was in his fevered heart, and pained it,
   Till it ached for joys she must deny.
      But the maiden's fears
      Stayed him, till in tears
   On the bed he sank, with sobbing cry.

XVI.

And she leans above him—"Dear one, still thee!
   Ah, how sad am I to see thee so!
But, alas! these limbs of mine would chill thee:
   Love! they mantle not with passion's glow;
      Thou wouldst be afraid,
      Didst thou find the maid
   Thou hast chosen, cold as ice or snow."

XVII.

Round her waist his eager arms he bended,
   With the strength that youth and love inspire;
"Wert thou even from the grave ascended,
   I could warm thee well with my desire!"
      Panting kiss on kiss!
      Overflow of bliss!
   "Burn'st thou not, and feelest me on fire?"

XVIII.

Closer yet they cling, and intermingling,
    Tears and broken sobs proclaim the rest;
His hot breath through all her frame is tingling,
    There they lie, caressing and caressed.
        His impassioned mood
        Warms her torpid blood,
    Yet there beats no heart within her breast!

XIX.

Meanwhile goes the mother, softly creeping,
    Through the house, on needful cares intent,
Hears a murmur, and, while all are sleeping,
    Wonders at the sounds, and what they meant.
        Who was whispering so?—
        Voices soft and low,
    In mysterious converse strangely blent.

XX.

Straightway by the door herself she stations,
    There to be assured what was amiss;
And she hears love's fiery protestations,
    Words of ardour and endearing bliss:
        "Hark, the cock! 'Tis light!
        But to-morrow night
    Thou wilt come again?" and kiss on kiss.

XXI.

Quick the latch she raises, and, with features
    Anger-flushed, into the chamber hies.
"Are there in my house such shameless creatures,
    Minions to the stranger's will?" she cries.
        By the dying light,
           Who is't meets her sight?
God! 'tis her own daughter she espies!

XXII.

And the youth in terror sought to cover,
    With her own light veil, the maiden's head,
Clasped her close; but, gliding from her lover,
    Back the vestment from her brow she spread,
        And her form upright,
           As with ghostly might,
Long and slowly rises from the bed.

XXIII.

"Mother! mother! wherefore thus deprive me
    Of such joy as I this night have known?
Wherefore from these warm embraces drive me?
    Was I wakened up to meet thy frown?
        Did it not suffice
           That, in virgin guise,
To an early grave you forced me down?

XXIV.

"Fearful is the weird that forced me hither,
    From the dark-heaped chamber where I lay;
Powerless are your drowsy anthems, neither
    Can your priests prevail, howe'er they pray.
        Salt nor lymph can cool,
        Where the pulse is full;
    Love must still burn on, though wrapped in clay.

XXV.

"To this youth my early troth was plighted,
    Whilst yet Venus ruled within the land;
Mother! and that vow ye falsely slighted,
    At your new and gloomy faith's command.
        But no god will hear,
        If a mother swear
    Pure from love to keep her daughter's hand.

XXVI.

"Nightly from my narrow chamber driven,
    Come I to fulfil my destined part.
Him to seek to whom my troth was given,
    And to draw the life-blood from his heart.
        He hath served my will;
        More I yet must kill,
    For another prey I now depart.

XXVII.

"Fair young man! thy thread of life is broken,
    Human skill can bring no aid to thee.
There thou hast my chain—a ghastly token—
    And this lock of thine I take with me.
        Soon must thou decay,
        Soon wilt thou be gray,
    Dark although to-night thy tresses be!

XXVIII.

"Mother! hear, oh, hear my last entreaty!
    Let the funeral-pile arise once more;
Open up my wretched tomb for pity,
    And in flames our souls to peace restore.
        When the ashes glow,
        When the fire-sparks flow,
    To the ancient gods aloft we soar."

From *Thalaba the Destroyer*

ROBERT SOUTHEY   1801

The Eighth Book.

WOMAN.

Go not among the Tombs, Old Man!
There is a madman there.

OLD MAN.

Will he harm me if I go?

WOMAN.

Not he, poor miserable man!
But 'tis a wretched sight to see
His utter wretchedness.
For all day long he lies on a grave,
And never is he seen to weep,
And never is he heard to groan.
Nor ever at the hour of prayer
Bends his knee, nor moves his lips.
I have taken him food for charity
And never a word he spake,
But yet so ghastly he looked
That I have awakened at night
With the dream of his ghastly eyes.
Now go not among the Tombs, Old Man!

OLD MAN.

Wherefore has the wrath of God
So sorely stricken him?

WOMAN.

He came a Stranger to the land,
And did good service to the Sultan,
And well his service was rewarded.
The Sultan named him next himself,
And gave a palace for his dwelling,
And dowered his bride with rich domains.
But on his wedding night
There came the Angel of Death.
Since that hour a man distracted
Among the sepulchres he wanders.
The Sultan when he heard the tale
Said that for some untold crime
Judgement thus had stricken him,
And asking Heaven forgiveness
That he had shewn him favour,
Abandoned him to want.

OLD MAN.

A Stranger did you say?

WOMAN.

An Arab born, like you.
But go not among the Tombs,
For the sight of his wretchedness
Might make a hard heart ache!

OLD MAN.

Nay, nay, I never yet have shunned
A countryman in distress:
And the sound of his dear native tongue
May be like the voice of a friend.

>Then to the Sepulchre
>The Woman pointed out,
>Old Moath bent his way.
>By the tomb lay Thalaba,
>In the light of the setting eve.
>The sun, and the wind, and the rain
>Had rusted his raven locks,
>His cheeks were fallen in,
>His face bones prominent,
>By the tomb he lay along
>And his lean fingers played,

Unwitting, with the grass that grew beside.

>The Old Man knew him not,
>And drawing near him cried
>"Countryman, peace be with thee!"
>The sound of his dear native tongue
>Awakened Thalaba.
>He raised his countenance
>And saw the good Old Man,

And he arose, and fell upon his neck,

>And groaned in bitterness.
>Then Moath knew the youth,

And feared that he was childless, and he turned

His eyes, and pointed to the tomb.
"Old Man!" cried Thalaba,
"Thy search is ended there!"

The father's cheek grew white
And his lip quivered with the misery;
Howbeit, collecting with a painful voice
He answered, "God is good! his will be done!"

The woe in which he spake,
The resignation that inspired his speech,
They softened Thalaba.
"Thou hast a solace in thy grief," he cried,
"A comforter within!
"Moath! thou seest me here,
"Delivered to the Evil Powers,
"A God-abandoned wretch."

The Old Man looked at him incredulous.
"Nightly," the youth pursued,
"Thy daughter comes to drive me to despair.
"Moath thou thinkest me mad,…
"But when the Cryer from the Minaret
"Proclaims the midnight hour,
"Hast thou a heart to see her?"

In the Meidan now
The clang of clarions and of drums
Accompanied the Sun's descent.
"Dost thou not pray? my son!"
Said Moath, as he saw
The white flag waving on the neighbouring Mosque;

    Then Thalaba's eye grew wild,
 "Pray!" echoed he, "I must not pray!"
    And the hollow groan he gave
    Went to the Old Man's heart,
 And bowing down his face to earth,
In fervent agony he called on God.

    A night of darkness and of storms!
    Into the Chamber of the Tomb
        Thalaba led the Old Man,
        To roof him from the rain.
        A night of storms! the wind
        Swept thro' the moonless sky
And moaned among the pillared sepulchres.
    And in the pauses of its sweep
        They heard the heavy rain
    Beat on the monument above.
    In silence on Oneiza's grave
    The Father and the Husband sate.

    The Cryer from the Minaret
        Proclaimed the midnight hour;
        "Now! now!" cried Thalaba,
    And o'er the chamber of the tomb
        There spread a lurid gleam
Like the reflection of a sulphur fire,
    And in that hideous light
Oneiza stood before them, it was She,
Her very lineaments, and such as death
Had changed them, livid cheeks, and lips of blue.
    But in her eyes there dwelt

    Brightness more terrible
    Than all the loathsomeness of death.
     "Still art thou living, wretch?"
In hollow tones she cried to Thalaba,
    "And must I nightly leave my grave
     "To tell thee, still in vain,
     "God has abandoned thee?"

  "This is not she!" the Old Man exclaimed,
    "A Fiend! a manifest Fiend!"
  And to the youth he held his lance,
    "Strike and deliver thyself!"
    "Strike HER!" cried Thalaba,
    And palsied of all powers
Gazed fixedly upon the dreadful form.
  "Yea! strike her!" cried a voice whose tones
Flowed with such sudden healing thro' his soul,
    As when the desert shower
    From death delivered him.
But unobedient to that well-known voice
    His eye was seeking it,
    When Moath firm of heart,
Performed the bidding; thro' the vampire* corpse
    He thrust his lance; it fell,
    And howling with the wound
    Its demon tenant fled.
  A sapphire light fell on them,
And garmented with glory, in their sight
    Oneiza's Spirit stood.

"O Thalaba!" she cried,
"Abandon not thyself!
"Wouldst thou for ever lose me?... go, fulfill
"Thy quest, that in the Bowers of Paradise
"In vain I may not wait thee, O my Husband!"
    To Moath then the Spirit
Turned the dark lustre of her Angel eyes,
    "Short is thy destined path,
"O my dear father! to the abode of bliss.
    "Return to Araby,
        "There with the thought of death.
    "Comfort thy lonely age,
    "And Azrael the Deliverer, soon
        "Shall visit thee in peace."

    They stood with earnest eyes
    And arms out-reaching, when again
        The darkness closed around them.
    The soul of Thalaba revived;
    He from the floor the quiver took
    And as he bent the bow, exclaimed,
"Was it the over-ruling Providence
"That in the hour of frenzy led my hands
    "Instinctively to this?
"To-morrow, and the sun shall brace anew
"The slackened cord that now sounds loose and damp,
"To-morrow, and its livelier tone will sing
"In tort vibration to the arrow's flight.
"I... but I also, with recovered health
    "Of heart, shall do my duty.

"My Father! here I leave thee then!" he cried,
        "And not to meet again
        "Till at the gate of Paradise
"The eternal union of our joys commence.
"We parted last in darkness!"... and the youth
        Thought with what other hopes,
        But now his heart was calm,
For on his soul a heavenly hope had dawned.
The Old Man answered nothing, but he held
        His garment and to the door
        Of the Tomb Chamber followed him.
        The rain had ceased, the sky was wild
        Its black clouds broken by the storm.
        And lo! it chanced that in the chasm
        Of Heaven between, a star,
Leaving along its path continuous light,
Shot eastward. "See my guide!" quoth Thalaba,
        And turning, he received
        Old Moath's last embrace,
        And his last blessing.
            It was eve,
When an old Dervise, sitting in the sun
At his cell door, invited for the night
        The traveller; in the sun
        He spread the plain repast
Rice and fresh grapes, and at their feet there flowed
        The brook of which they drank.

        So as they sate at meal,
        With song, with music, and with dance,

   A wedding train went by;
   The veiled bride, the female slaves,
   The torches of festivity,
  And trump and timbrel merriment
    Accompanied their way.
    The good old Dervise gave
    A blessing as they past.
    But Thalaba looked on,
And breathed a low, deep groan, and hid his face.
The Dervise had known sorrow; and he felt
    Compassion; and his words
   Of pity and of piety
    Opened the young man's heart
    And he told all his tale.

"Repine not, O my Son!" the Old Man replied,
   "That Heaven has chastened thee.
"Behold this vine, I found it a wild tree
   "Whose wanton strength had swoln into
"Irregular twigs, and bold excrescencies,
"And spent itself in leaves and little rings,
"In the vain flourish of its outwardness
    "Wasting the sap and strength
    "That should have given forth fruit.
   "But when I pruned the Tree,
"Then it grew temperate in its vain expence
"Of useless leaves, and knotted, as thou seest,
"Into these full, clear, clusters, to repay
    "The hand whose foresight wounded it.
    "Repine not, O my Son!

"In wisdom and in mercy Heaven inflicts,
"Like a wise Leech, its painful remedies."

Then pausing, "whither goest thou now?" he asked.
    "I know not," answered Thalaba,
    "Straight on, with Destiny my guide."
Quoth the Old Man, "I will not blame thy trust,
    "And yet methinks thy feet
    "Should tread with certainty.
"In Kaf the Simorg hath his dwelling place,
"The all-knowing Bird of Ages, who hath seen
"The World, with all her children, thrice destroyed.
    "Long is the thither path,
"And difficult the way, of danger full;
    "But his unerring voice
"Could point to certain end thy weary search."

    Easy assent the youth
Gave to the words of wisdom; and behold
At dawn, the adventurer on his way to Kaf.
    And he has travelled many a day
    And many a river swum over,
    And many a mountain ridge has crost
    And many a measureless plain,
    And now amid the wilds advanced,
        Long is it since his eyes
        Have seen the trace of man.

    Cold! cold! 'tis a chilly clime
    That the toil of the youth has reached,
    And he is aweary now,

      And faint for the lack of food.
      Cold! cold! there is no Sun in heaven
      But a heavy and uniform cloud
      And the snows begin to fall.
Dost thou wish for thy deserts, O Son of Hodeirah?
      Dost thou long for the gales of Arabia?
      Cold! cold! his blood flows languid,
      His hands are red, his lips are blue,
      His feet are sore with the frost.
      Cheer thee! cheer thee! Thalaba!
        A little yet bear up!

      All waste! no sign of life
      But the track of the wolf and the bear!
      No sound but the wild, wild wind
      And the snow crunching under his feet!
      Night is come; no moon, no stars,
      Only the light of the snow!
      But behold a fire in the cave of the hill
      A heart-reviving fire;
      And thither with strength renewed
      Thalaba presses on.

      He found a Woman in the cave,
      A solitary Woman,
      Who by the fire was spinning
      And singing as she spun.
      The pine boughs they blazed chearfully
      And her face was bright with the flame.
      Her face was as a Damsel's face
      And yet her hair was grey.

She bade him welcome with a smile
And still continued spinning
And singing as she spun.
The thread the Woman drew
Was finer than the silkworm's,
Was finer than the gossamer.
The song she sung was low and sweet
And Thalaba knew not the words.

He laid his bow before the hearth,
For the string was frozen stiff.
He took the quiver from his neck,
For the arrow plumes were iced.
Then as the chearful fire
Revived his languid limbs,
The adventurer asked for food.
The Woman answered him,
And still her speech was song,
"The She Bear she dwells near to me,
"And she hath cubs, one, two and three.
"She hunts the deer and brings him here,
"And then with her I make good cheer,
        "And she to the chase is gone
        "And she will be here anon."

She ceased from her work as she spake,
And when she had answered him,
Again her fingers twirled the thread
And again the Woman began
In low, sweet, tones to sing
The unintelligible song.

The thread she spun it gleamed like gold
In the light of the odorous fire,
And yet so wonderous thin,
That save when the light shone on it
It could not be seen by the eye.
The youth sate watching it,
And she beheld his wonder.
And then again she spake to him
And still her speech was song,
"Now twine it round thy hands I say,
"Now twine it round thy hands I pray,
"My thread is small, my thread is fine,
    "But he must be
    "A stronger than thee,
"Who can break this thread of mine!"

And up she raised her bright blue eyes
And sweetly she smiled on him,
And he conceived no ill.
And round and round his right hand,
And round and round his left,
He wound the thread so fine.
And then again the Woman spake,
And still her speech was song,
"Now thy strength, O Stranger, strain,
"Now then break the slender chain."

Thalaba strove, but the thread
Was woven by magic hands,
And in his cheek the flush of shame
Arose, commixt with fear.

> She beheld and laughed at him,
> And then again she sung,
> "My thread is small, my thread is fine,
>> "But he must be
>> "A stronger than thee
> "Who can break this thread of mine."
>
> And up she raised her bright blue eyes
> And fiercely she smiled on him,
> "I thank thee, I thank thee, Hodeirah's Son!
> "I thank thee for doing what can't be undone,
> "For binding thyself in the chain I have spun!"
>> Then from his head she wrenched
>> A lock of his raven hair,
>> And cast it in the fire
>> And cried aloud as it burnt,
> "Sister! Sister! hear my voice!
> "Sister! Sister! come and rejoice,
>> "The web is spun,
>> "The prize is won,
>> "The work is done,
> "For I have made captive Hodeirah's Son."

...

Note

* In the *Lettres Juives* is the following extract from the *Mercure Historique et Politique*. Octob. 1736.

We have had in this country a new scene of Vampirism, which is duly attested by two officers of the Tribunal of *Belgrade*, who took cognizance of the affair on the spot, and by an officer in his Imperial Majesty's troops at *Gradisch* (*in Sclavonia*) who was an eye-witness of the proceedings.

In the beginning of *September* there died at the village of *Kisilova*, three leagues from *Gradisch*, an old man of above threescore and two: three days after he was buried he appeared in the night to his son, and desired he would give him somewhat to eat, and then disappeared. The next day the son told his neighbours these particulars. That night the Father did not come, but the next evening he made him another visit, and desired something to eat. It is not known whether his son gave him any thing or not, but the next morning the young man was found dead in his bed. The Magistrate or Bailiff of the place had notice of this, as also that the same day five or six persons fell sick in the village, and died one after the other. He sent an exact account of this to the tribunal of *Belgrade*, and thereupon two commissioners were dispatched to the village attended by an executioner, with instructions to examine closely into the affair. An officer in the Imperial service, from whom we have this relation, went also from *Gradisch*, in order to examine personally an affair of which he had heard so much. They opened in the first place the graves of all who had been buried in six weeks. When they came to that of the old man, they found his eyes open, his colour fresh, his respiration quick and strong, yet he appeared to be stiff and insensible. From these signs they concluded him to be a notorious *Vampire*. The executioner thereupon, by the command of the commissioners, struck a stake thro' his heart; and when he had so done, they made a bonfire, and therein consumed the carcase to ashes. There was no marks of Vampirism found on his son, or on the bodies of the other persons who died so suddenly.

Thanks be to God, we are as far as any people can be from giving into credulity, we acknowledge that all the lights of physick do not enable us to give any account of this fact, nor do we pretend to enter into its causes. However, we cannot avoid giving credit to a matter of fact juridically attested by competent and unsuspected witnesses, especially since it is far from being the only one of the kind. We shall here annex an instance of the same sort in 1732, already inserted in the *Gleaner*, No. 18.

In a certain town of *Hungary*, which is called in Latin *Oppida Heidonum*, on the other side *Tibiscus*, vulgarly called the *Teysse*; that is to say, the river which washes the celebrated territory of *Tokay* as also a part of *Transilvania*. The people known by the name of *Heydukes* believe that certain dead persons, whom they call Vampires, suck the blood of the living, insomuch that these people appear like skeletons, while the dead bodies of the suckers are so full of blood, that it runs out at all the passages of their bodies, and even at their very pores. This odd opinion of theirs they support by a multitude of facts attested in such a manner, that they leave no room for doubt. We shall here mention some of the most considerable.

It is now about five years ago, that a certain *Heyduke*, an inhabitant of the village of *Medreiga*, whose name was Arnold Paul, was bruised to death by a hay-cart, which ran over him. Thirty days after his death, no less than four persons died suddenly, in that manner, wherein, according to the tradition of the country, those people generally die who are sucked by Vampires. Upon this a story was called to mind, that this *Arnold Paul* had told in his life-time, viz: that at *Cossova* on the Frontiers of the *Turkish Servia*, he had been tormented by a Vampire; (now the established opinion is that a person sucked by a Vampire, becomes a Vampire himself, and sucks in his turn.) But that he had found a way to rid himself of this evil, by eating some of the earth out of the Vampire's grave, and rubbing himself with his blood. This precaution however did not hinder his becoming a Vampire; insomuch that his body being taken up forty days after his death, all the marks of a notorious Vampire were found thereon. His complexion was fresh, his hair, nails and beard were grown; he was full of fluid blood, which ran from all parts of his body upon his shroud. The *Hadnagy* or *Bailiff* of the place, who was a person well acquainted with Vampirism, caused a sharp stake to be thrust, as the custom is, through the heart of *Arnold Paul*, and also quite through his body; whereupon he cried out dreadfully as if he had been alive. This done, they cut off his head, burnt his body, and threw the ashes thereof into *Saave*. They took the same measures with the bodies of those persons who had died of Vampirism, for fear that they should fall to sucking in their turns.

All these prudent steps did not hinder the same mischief from breaking out again about five years afterwards, when several people in the same village died in a very odd manner. In the space of three months, seventeen persons of all ages and sexes died of Vampirism, some suddenly, and some after two or three days suffering. Amongst others there was one *Stanoska*, the daughter of a *Heyduke* whose name was *Jovitzo* who going to bed in perfect health, waked in the middle of the night, and making a terrible outcry, affirmed that the son of a certain *Heyduke* whose name was *Millo*, and who had been dead about three weeks, had attempted to strangle her in her sleep. She continued from that time in a languishing condition, and in the space of three days died. What this girl had said discovered the son of *Millo* to be a Vampire. They took up the body and found him so in effect. The principal persons of the place, particularly the Physician and Surgeons, began to examine very narrowly, how, in spite of all their precautions, Vampirism had again broke out in so terrible a manner. After a strict inquisition, they found that the deceased *Arnold Paul* had not only sucked the four persons before mentioned, but likewise several beasts, of whom the new Vampires had eaten, particularly the son of *Millo*. Induced by these circumstances, they took a resolution, of digging up the bodies of all persons who had died within a certain time. They did so, and amongst forty bodies, there were found seventeen evidently Vampires. Through the hearts of these they drove stakes, cut off their heads, burnt the bodies, and threw the ashes into the river. All the informations we have been speaking of were taken in a legal way, and all the executions were so performed, as appears by certificates drawn up in full form, attested by several officers in the neighbouring garrisons, by the surgeons of several Regiments, and the principal inhabitants of the place. The verbal process was sent towards the latter end of last *January* to the council of war at *Vienna*, who thereupon established a special commission to examine into these facts. Those just now mentioned were attested by the *Hadnagi Barriarer*, the principal *Heyduke* of the village, as also by *Battuer*, first Lieutenant of Prince *Alexander* of *Wirtemberg*, *Flickstenger*, surgeon major of the regiment of *Furstemberg*, three other surgeons of the same regiment, and several other persons.

A similar superstition prevails in Greece. The man whose story we are going to relate, was a Peasant of Mycone, naturally ill natured and quarrelsome, this is a circumstance to be taken notice of in such cases. He was murdered in the fields, nobody knew how, or by whom. Two days after his being buried in a Chapel in the town, it was noised about that he was seen to walk in the night with great haste, that he tumbled about people's goods, put out their lamps, griped them behind, and a thousand other monkey tricks. At first the story was received with laughter; but the thing was looked upon to be serious when the better sort of people began to complain of it; the Papas themselves gave credit to the fact, and no doubt had their reasons for so doing; masses must be said, to be sure: but for all this, the Peasant drove his old trade and heeded nothing they could do. After divers meetings of the chief people of the city, of priests, and monks, it was gravely concluded, that 'twas necessary in consequence of some musty ceremonial to wait till nine days after the interment should be expired.

On the tenth day they said one mass in the chapel where the body was laid, in order to drive out the Demon which they imagined was got into it. After mass they took up the body, and got every thing ready for pulling out its heart. The butcher of the town, an old clumsy fellow, first opens the belly instead of the breast, he groped a long while among the entrails, but could not find what he looked for; at last somebody told him he should cut up the Diaphragm. The heart was then pulled out, to the admiration of all the spectators. In the mean time the Corpse stunk so abominably that they were obliged to burn frankincense; but the smoke mixing with the exhalations from the carcass increased the stink, and began to muddle the poor people's pericranies. Their imagination, struck with the spectacle before them, grew full of visions. It came into their noddles, that a thick smoke came out of the body; we durst not say 'twas the smoke of the incense. They were incessantly bawling out Vroucolacas in the chapel and place before it; this is the name they give to these pretended Redivivi. The noise bellowed thro' the streets, and it seemed to be a name invented on purpose to rend the roof of the chapel. Several there present averr'd that the wretches blood was extremely red; the Butcher swore the body was still warm, whence they concluded that the Deceas'd was a very ill man for not being thoroughly dead, or in plain terms for suffering himself to be re-animated by Old Nick; which is the notion they have of Vroucolacas. They then roar'd out that name in a stupendous manner. Just at this time came in a flock of people loudly protesting they plainly perceived the Body was not grown stiff when it was carried from the fields to Church to be buried, and that consequently it was a true Vroucolacas; which word was still the burden of the song.

I don't doubt they would have sworn it did not stink, had not we been there; so mazed were the poor people with this disaster, and so infatuated with their notion of the Dead being re-animated. As for us, who were got as close to the corpse as we could, that we might be more exact in our observations, we were almost poisoned with the intolerable stink that issued from it. When they asked us what we thought of this body, we told them we believed it to be very thoroughly dead: but as we were willing to cure, or at least not to exasperate their prejudiced imaginations, we represented to them, that it was no wonder the butcher should feel a little warmth when he groped among Entrails that were then rotting, that it was no extraordinary thing for it to emit fumes, since dung turned up will do the same; that as for the pretended redness of the blood, it still appeared by the butcher's hands to be nothing but a very stinking nasty smear.

After all our reasons they were of opinion it would be their wisest course to burn the dead man's heart on the sea-shore: but this execution did not make him a bit more tractable; he went on with his racket more furiously than ever; he was accused of beating folks in the night, breaking down doors, and even roofs of houses, clattering windows, tearing clothes, emptying bottles and vessels. 'Twas the most thirsty Devil! I believe he did not spare any body but the Consul in whose house we lodged. Nothing could be more miserable than the condition of this island; all the inhabitants seemed frighted out of their senses: the wisest among them were stricken like the rest; 'twas an epidemical disease of the brain, as dangerous and infectious as the madness of dogs. Whole families quitted their houses, and brought their tent beds from the farthest parts of the town into the public place, there to spend the night. They were every instant complaining of some new insult; nothing was to be heard but sighs and groans at the approach of night: the better sort of people retired into the country.

When the prepossession was so general, we thought it our best way to hold our tongues. Had we opposed it, we had not only been accounted ridiculous blockheads, but Atheists and Infidels, how was it possible to stand against the madness of a whole people? Those that believed we doubted the truth of the fact, came and upbraided us with our incredulity, and strove to prove that there were such things as Vroucolacasses, by citations out of the Buckler of Faith, written by F. Richard a Jesuit Missionary. He was a Latin, say they, and consequently you ought to give him credit. We should have got nothing by denying the justness of the consequence: it was as good as a Comedy to us every morning to hear the new follies committed by this night bird; they charged him with being guilty of the most abominable sins.

Some Citizens, that were most zealous for the good of the public, fancied they had been deficient in the most material part of the ceremony. They were of opinion that they had been wrong in saying mass before they had pulled out the wretches heart: had we taken this precaution, quoth they, we had bit the Devil as sure as a gun; he would have been hanged before he would ever have come there again: whereas saying mass first, the cunning Dog fled for it awhile and came back again when the danger was over.

Notwithstanding these wise reflections, they remained in as much perplexity as they were the first day: they meet night and morning, they debate, they make professions three days and three nights, they oblige the Papas to fast; you might see them running from house to house, holy-water-brush in hand sprinkling it all about, and washing the doors with it; nay they poured it into the mouth of the poor Vroucolacas.

We so often repeated it to the Magistrates of the town, that in Xtendom we should keep the strictest watch a nights upon such an occasion, to observe what was done; that at last they caught a few vagabonds, who undoubtedly had a hand in these disorders: but either they were not the chief ringleaders, or else they were released too soon. For two days afterwards, to make themselves amends for the Lent they had kept in prison, they fell foul again upon the wine tubs of those who were such fools as to leave their houses empty in the night: so that the people were forced to betake themselves again to their prayers.

One day as they were hard at this work, after having stuck I know not how many naked swords over the grave of this corpse, which they took up three or four times a day, for any man's whim; an Albaneze that happened to be at Mycone, took upon him to say with a voice of authority, that it was to the last degree ridiculous to make use of the swords of Xtians in a case like this. Can you not conceive, blind as ye are, says he, that the handles of these swords being made like a cross, hinders the Devil from coming out of the body? Why do you not rather take the Turkish sabres? The advice of this learned man had no effect: the Vroucolacas was incorrigible, and all the inhabitants were in a strange consternation; they knew not now what Saint to call upon, when of a sudden with one voice, as if they had given each other the hint, they fell to bawling out all thro' the city, that it was intolerable to wait any longer; that the only way left was to burn the Vroucolacas intire; that after so doing, let the Devil lurk in it if he could; that 'twas better to have recourse to this extremity than to have the island totally deserted, and indeed whole families began to pack up, in order to retire to Syre or Tinos. The magistrates therefore ordered the Vroucolacas to be carryed to the point of the island St. George, where they prepared a great pile with pitch and tar, for fear the wood, as dry as it was, should not burn fast enough of itself. What they had before left of this miserable carcass was thrown into this fire and consumed presently: 'twas on the first of January, 1701. We saw the flame as we returned from Delos; it might justly be called a bonfire of joy, since after this no more complaints were heard against the Vroucolacas; they said that the Devil had now met with his match, and some ballads were made to turn him into ridicule.

Tournefort.

The Dark Ladie

ANNE BANNERMAN 1802

The knights return'd from Holy Land,
Sir Guyon led the armed train;
And to his castle, on the sea,
He welcom'd them again.

He welcom'd them with soldier glee,
And sought to charm away their toil;
But none, on Guyon's clouded face,
Had ever seen a smile!

And, as the hour of eve drew on,
That clouded face more dark became,
No burst of mirth could overpow'r
The shiverings of his frame;

And often to the banner'd door
His straining eyes, unbidden, turn'd;
Above, around, they glanced wild,
But ever there return'd.

At every pause, all breathless then,
And pale as death, he bent his ear,
Tho' not a sound the silence broke,
He seemed still to hear!

And when the feast was spread, and all
The guests, assembled, were at meat,
There pass'd them by, with measur'd step,
And took the upper seat,
A Ladie, clad in ghastly white,
And veiled to the feet:

She spoke not when she enter'd there;
She spoke not when the feast was done;
And every knight, in chill amaze,
Survey'd her one by one:

For thro' the foldings of her veil,
Her long black veil that swept the ground,
A light was seen to dart from eyes
That mortal never own'd.

And then the knights on Guyon turn'd
Their fixed gaze, and shudder'd now;
For smother'd fury seem'd to bring
The dew-drops on his brow.

But, from the Ladie in the veil,
Their eyes they could not long withdraw,
And when they tried to speak, that glare
Still kept them mute with awe!

Each wish'd to rouse his failing heart,
Yet look'd and trembled all, the while;
All, till the midnight clock had toll'd
Its summons from the southern aisle.

And when the last dull stroke had rung,
And left behind its deep'ning knell,
The Ladie rose, and fill'd with wine,
Fill'd to the brim, the sparkling shell.

And to the' alarmed guests she turn'd,
No breath was heard, no voice, no sound,
And in a tone, so deadly deep,
She pledg'd them all around,
That in their hearts, and thro' their limbs,
No pulses could be found.

And, when their senses back return'd,
They gaz'd upon the steps of stone
On which the Dark Ladie had stood,
They gaz'd... but she was gone!...

Then Guyon rose,... and ah! to rest,
When every weary knight was led,
After what they had seen and heard,
What wonder, slumber fled!

For, often as they turn'd to rest,
And sleep prest down each heavy eye,
Before them, in her black veil wrapt,
They saw the Dark Ladie.

And then the voice, the tone, that stopt
Thro' all their limbs, the rushing blood;
The cup which she had fill'd with wine,
The steps on which she stood.

The sound, the tone,... no human voice
Could ever reach that echo, deep;
And, ever as they turn'd to rest,
It roused them from sleep!...

The morning dawns... the knights are met,
And seated in the arched hall,
And some were loud, and some spoke low,
But Huart none at all!

"Dost not remember, well, cries one,
When wide the sacred banners flew,
And when, beneath the blessed Cross,
The infidels we slew.

"This same Sir Guyon, erst so brave,
In fight, who ever led the van,
Soon as the Sepulchre he saw,
Grew pale and trembled then?

"And as the kneeling knights ador'd,
And wept around that holy place,
O God! I've seen the big drops burst
For hours upon his face!

"And when I named the blessed name,
His face became as livid clay,
And, on his foamy lips, the sounds,
Unutter'd, died away!"

"But O! that Ladie! Huart cries,...
That Ladie, with the long black veil,

This morn I heard!... I hear it still,
The lamentable tale!

"I hear the hoary-headed man,
I kept him till the morning dawn,
For five unbroken hours he talk'd,
With me they were as one!

"He told me he had lived long
Within this castle, on the sea;
But peace, O Heaven! he never had,
Since he saw the Dark Ladie!

"'Twas chill," he said, "a hazy night,
Just as the light began to fail,
Sir Guyon came and brought with him
The Ladie in the veil:

"Yes! to this castle on the sea,
The wild surge dashing on its base,
He brought her in that frightful veil
That ever hides her face.

"And many a time, he said, he tried
That ne'er-uncover'd face to see:
At eve and more, at noon and night;
But still it could not be!

"Till once! but O! that glaring eye,
It dried the life-blood, working here!
And when he turn'd to look again,
The Ladie was not near!

"But, sometimes, thro' her curtain'd tower,
A strange uncolour'd light was seen,
And something, of unearthly hue,
Still passed on between:

"And then aloof its clasped hands
Were wrung, and tossed to and fro!
And sounds came forth, dull, deep, and wild,
And O! how deadly slow!

"He quak'd to tell!... But, never more,
In quiet sleep, he rested long;
For still, on his alarmed ear,
That rousing echo rung!

"It glar'd for ever on his sight,
That fixed eye, so wildly keen!
Till life became a heavy load;
And long had heavy been.

"He told me that, at last, he heard
Some story, how this poor Ladie
Had left, alas! her husband's home
With this dread knight to flee:

"And how her sinking heart recoil'd,
And how her throbbing bosom beat,
And how sensation almost left
Her cold convulsed feet:

"And how she clasp'd her little son,
Before she tore herself away;

And how she turn'd again to bless
The cradle where he lay.

"But where Sir Guyon took her then,
Ah! none could ever hear or know,
Or, why, beneath that long black veil,
Her wild eyes sparkle so.

"Or whence those deep unearthly tones,
That human bosom never own'd;
Or why, it cannot be remov'd,
That folded veil that sweeps the ground?"

The Vampyre

JOHN STAGG   1810

"Why looks my lord so deadly pale?
    Why fades the crimson from his cheek?
What can my dearest husband ail?
    Thy heartfelt cares, O Herman, speak!

"Why, at the silent hour of rest,
    Dost thou in sleep so sadly mourn?
Has tho' with heaviest grief oppress'd,
    Griefs too distressful to be borne.

"Why heaves thy breast?—why throbs thy heart?
    O speak! and if there be relief
Thy Gertrude solace shall impart,
    If not, at least shall share thy grief.

"Wan is that cheek, which once the bloom
    Of manly beauty sparkling shew'd;
Dim are those eyes, in pensive gloom,
    That late with keenest lustre glow'd.

"Say why, too, at the midnight hour,
    You sadly pant and tug for breath,
As if some supernat'ral pow'r
    Were pulling you away to death?

"Restless, tho' sleeping, still you groan,
    And with convulsive horror start;
O Herman! to thy wife make known
    That grief which preys upon thy heart."

"O Gertrude! how shall I relate
    Th' uncommon anguish that I feel;
Strange as severe is this my fate,—
    A fate I cannot long conceal.

"In spite of all my wonted strength,
    Stern destiny has seal'd my doom;
The dreadful malady at length
    Wil drag me to the silent tomb!"

"But say, my Herman, what's the cause
    Of this distress, and all thy care.
That, vulture-like, thy vitals gnaws,
    And galls thy bosom with despair?

"Sure this can be no common grief,
    Sure this can be no common pain?
Speak, if this world contain relief,
    That soon thy Gertrude shall obtain."

"O Gertrude, 'tis a horrid cause,
    O Gertrude, 'tis unusual care,
That, vulture-like, my vitals gnaws,
    And galls my bosom with despair.

"Young Sigismund, my once dear friend,
    But lately he resign'd his breath;
With others I did him attend
    Unto the silent house of death.

"For him I wept, for him I mourn'd,
    Paid all to friendship that was due;
But sadly friendship is return'd,
    Thy Herman he must follow too!

"Must follow to the gloomy grave,
    In spite of human art or skill;
No pow'r on earth my life can save,
    'Tis fate's unalterable will!

"Young Sigismund, my once dear friend,
    But now my persecutor foul,
Doth his malevolence extend
    E'en to the torture of my soul.

"By night, when, wrapt in soundest sleep,
    All mortals share a soft repose,
My soul doth dreadful vigils keep,
    More keen than which hell scarely knows.

"From the drear mansion of the tomb,
    From the low regions of the dead,
The ghost of Sigismund doth roam,
    And dreadful haunts me in my bed!

"There, vested in infernal guise,
    (By means to me not understood,)
Close to my side the goblin lies,
    And drinks away my vital blood!

"Sucks from my veins the streaming life,
    And drains the fountain of my heart!
O Gertrude, Gertrude! dearest wife!
    Unutterable is my smart.

"When surfeited, the goblin dire,
    With banqueting by suckled gore,
Will to his sepulchre retire,
    Till night invites him forth once more.

"Then will he dreadfully return,
    And from my veins life's juices drain;
Whilst, slumb'ring, I with anguish mourn,
    And toss with agonizing pain!

"Already I'm exhausted, spent;
    His carnival is nearly o'er,
My soul with agony is rent,
    To-morrow I shall be no more!

"But, O my Gertrude! dearest wife!
    The keenest pangs hath last remain'd—
When dead, I too shall seek thy life,
    Thy blood by Herman shall be drain'd!

"But to avoid this horrid fate,
    Soon as I'm dead and laid in earth,
Drive thro' my corpse a jav'lin straight;—
    This shall prevent my coming forth.

"O watch with me, this last sad night,
    Watch in your chamber here alone,
But carefully conceal the light
    Until you hear my parting groan.

"Then at what time the vesper-bell
    Of yonder convent shall be toll'd,
That peal shall ring my passing knell,
    And Herman's body shall be cold!

"Then, and just then, thy lamp make bare,
    The starting ray, the bursting light,
Shall from my side the goblin scare,
    And shew him visible to sight!"

The live-long night poor Gertrude sate,
    Watch'd by her sleeping, dying lord;
The live-long night she mourn'd his fate,
    The object whom her soul ador'd.

Then at what time the vesper-bell
    Of yonder convent sadly toll'd,
Then, then was peal'd his passing knell,
    The hapless Herman he was cold!

Just at that moment Gertrude drew
    From 'neath her cloak the hidden light;
When, dreadful! she beheld in view
    The shade of Sigismund!—sad sight!

Indignant roll'd his ireful eyes,
    That gleam'd with wild horrific stare;
And fix'd a moment with surprise,
    Beheld aghast th' enlight'ning glare.

His jaws cadaverous were besmear'd
    With clott'd carnage o'er and o'er,
And all his horrid whole appear'd
    Distent, and fill'd with human gore!

With hideous scowl the spectre fled;
    She shriek'd aloud;—then swoon'd away!
The hapless Herman in his bed,
    All pale, a lifeless body lay!

Next day in council 'twas decreed,
    (Urg'd at the instance of the state,)
That shudd'ring nature should be freed
    From pests like these ere 'twas too late.

The choir then burst the fun'ral dome
    Where Sigismund was lately laid,
And found him, tho' within the tomb,
    Still warm as life, and undecay'd.

With blood his visage was distain'd,
    Ensanguin'd were his frightful eyes,
Each sign of former life remain'd,
    Save that all motionless he lies.

The corpse of Herman they contrive
    To the same sepulchre to take,
And thro' both carcases they drive,
    Deep in the earth, a sharpen'd stake!

By this was finish'd their career,
    Thro' this no longer they can roam;
From them their friends have nought to fear,
    Both quiet keep the slumb'ring tomb.

From *The Giaour*

LORD BYRON   1813

No breath of air to break the wave
That rolls below the Athenian's grave,
That tomb which, gleaming o'er the cliff,
First greets the homeward-veering skiff
High o'er the land he saved in vain;
When shall such Hero live again?

   Fair clime! where every season smiles
Benignant o'er those blessed isles,
Which, seen from far Colonna's height,
Make glad the heart that hails the sight,
And lend to loneliness delight.
There mildly dimpling, Ocean's cheek
Reflects the tints of many a peak
Caught by the laughing tides that lave
These Edens of the eastern wave:
And if at times a transient breeze
Break the blue crystal of the seas,
Or sweep one blossom from the trees,
How welcome is each gentle air
That wakes and wafts the odours there!
For there the Rose, o'er crag or vale,
Sultana of the Nightingale,
   The maid for whom his melody,
   His thousand songs are heard on high,

Blooms blushing to her lover's tale:
His queen, the garden queen, his Rose,
Unbent by winds, unchilled by snows,
Far from the winters of the west,
By every breeze and season blest,
Returns the sweets by Nature given
In softest incense back to Heaven;
And grateful yields that smiling sky
Her fairest hue and fragrant sigh.
And many a summer flower is there,
And many a shade that Love might share,
And many a grotto, meant for rest,
That holds the pirate for a guest;
Whose bark in sheltering cove below
Lurks for the passing peaceful prow,
Till the gay mariner's guitar
Is heard, and seen the Evening Star;
Then stealing with the muffled oar,
Far shaded by the rocky shore,
Rush the night-prowlers on the prey,
And turn to groans his roundelay.
Strange—that where Nature loved to trace,
As if for Gods, a dwelling place,
And every charm and grace hath mixed
Within the Paradise she fixed,
There man, enamoured of distress,
Should mar it into wilderness,
And trample, brute-like, o'er each flower
That tasks not one laborious hour;
Nor claims the culture of his hand

To bloom along the fairy land,
But springs as to preclude his care,
And sweetly woos him—but to spare!
Strange—that where all is Peace beside,
There Passion riots in her pride,
And Lust and Rapine wildly reign
To darken o'er the fair domain.
It is as though the Fiends prevailed
Against the Seraphs they assailed,
And, fixed on heavenly thrones, should dwell
The freed inheritors of Hell;
So soft the scene, so formed for joy,
So curst the tyrants that destroy!

   He who hath bent him o'er the dead
Ere the first day of Death is fled,
The first dark day of Nothingness,
The last of Danger and Distress,
(Before Decay's effacing fingers
Have swept the lines where Beauty lingers,)
And marked the mild angelic air,
The rapture of Repose that's there,
The fixed yet tender traits that streak
The languor of the placid cheek,
And—but for that sad shrouded eye,
   That fires not, wins not, weeps not, now,
   And but for that chill, changeless brow,
   Where cold Obstruction's apathy
   Appals the gazing mourner's heart,
   As if to him it could impart

The doom he dreads, yet dwells upon;
Yes, but for these and these alone,
Some moments, aye, one treacherous hour,
He still might doubt the Tyrant's power;
So fair, so calm, so softly sealed,
The first, last look by Death revealed!
Such is the aspect of this shore;
'Tis Greece, but living Greece no more!
So coldly sweet, so deadly fair,
We start, for Soul is wanting there.
Hers is the loveliness in death,
That parts not quite with parting breath;
But beauty with that fearful bloom,
That hue which haunts it to the tomb,
Expression's last receding ray,
A gilded Halo hovering round decay,
The farewell beam of Feeling past away!
Spark of that flame, perchance of heavenly birth,
Which gleams, but warms no more its cherished earth!

...

No more her sorrows I bewail,
Yet this will be a mournful tale,
And they who listen may believe,
Who heard it first had cause to grieve.

    Far, dark, along the blue sea glancing,
The shadows of the rocks advancing
Start on the fisher's eye like boat
Of island-pirate or Mainote;

And fearful for his light caïque,
He shuns the near but doubtful creek:
Though worn and weary with his toil,
And cumbered with his scaly spoil,
Slowly, yet strongly, plies the oar,
Till Port Leone's safer shore
Receives him by the lovely light
That best becomes an Eastern night.

  Who thundering comes on blackest steed,
With slackened bit and hoof of speed?
Beneath the clattering iron's sound
The caverned Echoes wake around
In lash for lash, and bound for bound:
The foam that streaks the courser's side
Seems gathered from the Ocean-tide:
Though weary waves are sunk to rest,
There's none within his rider's breast;
And though to-morrow's tempest lower,
'Tis calmer than thy heart, young Giaour!
I know thee not, I loathe thy race,
But in thy lineaments I trace
What Time shall strengthen, not efface:
Though young and pale, that sallow front
Is scathed by fiery Passion's brunt;
Though bent on earth thine evil eye,
As meteor-like thou glidest by,
Right well I view and deem thee one
Whom Othman's sons should slay or shun.

On—on he hastened, and he drew
My gaze of wonder as he flew:
Though like a Demon of the night
He passed, and vanished from my sight,
His aspect and his air impressed
A troubled memory on my breast,
And long upon my startled ear
Rung his dark courser's hoofs of fear.
He spurs his steed; he nears the steep,
That, jutting, shadows o'er the deep;
He winds around; he hurries by;
The rock relieves him from mine eye;
For, well I ween, unwelcome he
Whose glance is fixed on those that flee;
And not a star but shines too bright
On him who takes such timeless flight.
He wound along; but ere he passed
One glance he snatched, as if his last,
A moment checked his wheeling steed,
A moment breathed him from his speed,
A moment on his stirrup stood—
Why looks he o'er the olive wood?
The Crescent glimmers on the hill,
The Mosque's high lamps are quivering still
Though too remote for sound to wake
In echoes of the far tophaike,
The flashes of each joyous peal
Are seen to prove the Moslem's zeal.
To-night, set Rhamazani's sun;
To-night, the Bairam feast's begun;

To-night—but who and what art thou
Of foreign garb and fearful brow?
And what are these to thine or thee,
That thou shouldst either pause or flee?

 He stood—some dread was on his face,
Soon Hatred settled in its place:
It rose not with the reddening flush
Of transient Anger's hasty blush,
But pale as marble o'er the tomb,
Whose ghastly whiteness aids its gloom.
His brow was bent, his eye was glazed;
He raised his arm, and fiercely raised,
And sternly shook his hand on high,
As doubting to return or fly;
Impatient of his flight delayed,
Here loud his raven charger neighed—
Down glanced that hand, and grasped his blade;
That sound had burst his waking dream,
As Slumber starts at owlet's scream.
The spur hath lanced his courser's sides;
Away—away—for life he rides:
Swift as the hurled on high jerreed
Springs to the touch his startled steed;
The rock is doubled, and the shore
Shakes with the clattering tramp no more;
The crag is won, no more is seen
His Christian crest and haughty mien.
'Twas but an instant he restrained
That fiery barb so sternly reined;

'Twas but a moment that he stood,
Then sped as if by Death pursued;
But in that instant o'er his soul
Winters of Memory seemed to roll,
And gather in that drop of time
A life of pain, an age of crime.
O'er him who loves, or hates, or fears,
Such moment pours the grief of years:
What felt he then, at once opprest
By all that most distracts the breast?
That pause, which pondered o'er his fate,
Oh, who its dreary length shall date!
Though in Time's record nearly nought,
It was Eternity to Thought!
For infinite as boundless space
The thought that Conscience must embrace,
Which in itself can comprehend
Woe without name, or hope, or end.

   The hour is past, the Giaour is gone:
And did he fly or fall alone?
Woe to that hour he came or went!
The curse for Hassan's sin was sent
To turn a palace to a tomb;
He came, he went, like the Simoom,
That harbinger of Fate and gloom,
Beneath whose widely-wasting breath
  The very cypress droops to death—
Dark tree, still sad when others' grief is fled,
The only constant mourner o'er the dead!

    The steed is vanished from the stall;
No serf is seen in Hassan's hall;
The lonely Spider's thin gray pall
Waves slowly widening o'er the wall;
The Bat builds in his Haram bower,
And in the fortress of his power
The Owl usurps the beacon-tower;
The wild-dog howls o'er the fountain's brim,
With baffled thirst, and famine, grim;
For the stream has shrunk from its marble bed,
Where the weeds and the desolate dust are spread.
    'Twas sweet of yore to see it play
And chase the sultriness of day,
As springing high the silver dew
In whirls fantastically flew,
And flung luxurious coolness round
The air, and verdure o'er the ground.
'Twas sweet, when cloudless stars were bright,
To view the wave of watery light,
And hear its melody by night.
And oft had Hassan's Childhood played
Around the verge of that cascade;
And oft upon his mother's breast
That sound had harmonized his rest;
And oft had Hassan's Youth along
Its bank been soothed by Beauty's song;
And softer seemed each melting tone
Of Music mingled with its own.
But ne'er shall Hassan's Age repose
Along the brink at Twilight's close:

The stream that filled that font is fled—
The blood that warmed his heart is shed!
And here no more shall human voice
Be heard to rage, regret, rejoice.
The last sad note that swelled the gale
Was woman's wildest funeral wail:
That quenched in silence, all is still,
But the lattice that flaps when the wind is shrill:
Though raves the gust, and floods the rain,
No hand shall close its clasp again.
On desert sands 'twere joy to scan
The rudest steps of fellow man,
So here the very voice of Grief
Might wake an Echo like relief—
At least 'twould say, "All are not gone;
There lingers Life, though but in one"—
For many a gilded chamber's there,
Which Solitude might well forbear;
Within that dome as yet Decay
Hath slowly worked her cankering way—
But gloom is gathered o'er the gate,
Nor there the Fakir's self will wait;
Nor there will wandering Dervise stay,
For Bounty cheers not his delay;
Nor there will weary stranger halt
To bless the sacred "bread and salt."
    Alike must Wealth and Poverty
    Pass heedless and unheeded by,
    For Courtesy and Pity died
    With Hassan on the mountain side.

    His roof, that refuge unto men,
    Is Desolation's hungry den.
The guest flies the hall, and the vassal from labour,
Since his turban was cleft by the infidel's sabre!

    I hear the sound of coming feet,
    But not a voice mine ear to greet;
    More near—each turban I can scan,
    And silver-sheathèd ataghan;
    The foremost of the band is seen
    An Emir by his garb of green:
"Ho! who art thou?"—"This low salam
Replies of Moslem faith I am."
"The burthen ye so gently bear,
Seems one that claims your utmost care,
And, doubtless, holds some precious freight—
My humble bark would gladly wait."

    "Thou speakest sooth: thy skiff unmoor,
And waft us from the silent shore;
Nay, leave the sail still furled, and ply
The nearest oar that's scattered by,
And midway to those rocks where sleep
The channelled waters dark and deep.
Rest from your task—so—bravely done,
Our course has been right swiftly run;
Yet 'tis the longest voyage, I trow,
That one of— * * * "

    Sullen it plunged, and slowly sank,
The calm wave rippled to the bank;

I watched it as it sank, methought
Some motion from the current caught
Bestirred it more,—'twas but the beam
That checkered o'er the living stream:
I gazed, till vanishing from view,
Like lessening pebble it withdrew;
Still less and less, a speck of white
That gemmed the tide, then mocked the sight;
And all its hidden secrets sleep,
Known but to Genii of the deep,
Which, trembling in their coral caves,
They dare not whisper to the waves.

   As rising on its purple wing
The insect-queen of Eastern spring,
O'er emerald meadows of Kashmeer
Invites the young pursuer near,
And leads him on from flower to flower
A weary chase and wasted hour,
Then leaves him, as it soars on high,
With panting heart and tearful eye:
So Beauty lures the full-grown child,
With hue as bright, and wing as wild:
A chase of idle hopes and fears,
Begun in folly, closed in tears.
If won, to equal ills betrayed,
Woe waits the insect and the maid;
A life of pain, the loss of peace;
From infant's play, and man's caprice:
The lovely toy so fiercely sought

Hath lost its charm by being caught,
For every touch that wooed its stay
Hath brushed its brightest hues away,
Till charm, and hue, and beauty gone,
'Tis left to fly or fall alone.
With wounded wing, or bleeding breast,
Ah! where shall either victim rest?
Can this with faded pinion soar
From rose to tulip as before?
Or Beauty, blighted in an hour,
Find joy within her broken bower?
No: gayer insects fluttering by
Ne'er droop the wing o'er those that die,
And lovelier things have mercy shown
To every failing but their own,
And every woe a tear can claim
Except an erring Sister's shame.

The Mind, that broods o'er guilty woes,
   Is like the Scorpion girt by fire;
In circle narrowing as it glows,
The flames around their captive close,
Till inly searched by thousand throes,
   And maddening in her ire,
One sad and sole relief she knows—
The sting she nourished for her foes,
Whose venom never yet was vain,
Gives but one pang, and cures all pain,
And darts into her desperate brain:
So do the dark in soul expire,

Or live like Scorpion girt by fire;
So writhes the mind Remorse hath riven,
Unfit for earth, undoomed for heaven,
Darkness above, despair beneath,
Around it flame, within it death!

   Black Hassan from the Haram flies,
Nor bends on woman's form his eyes;
The unwonted chase each hour employs,
Yet shares he not the hunter's joys.
Not thus was Hassan wont to fly
When Leila dwelt in his Serai.
Doth Leila there no longer dwell?
That tale can only Hassan tell:
Strange rumours in our city say
Upon that eve she fled away
When Rhamazan's last sun was set,
And flashing from each Minaret
Millions of lamps proclaimed the feast
Of Bairam through the boundless East.
'Twas then she went as to the bath,
Which Hassan vainly searched in wrath;
For she was flown her master's rage
In likeness of a Georgian page,
And far beyond the Moslem's power
Had wronged him with the faithless Giaour.
Somewhat of this had Hassan deemed;
But still so fond, so fair she seemed,
Too well he trusted to the slave
Whose treachery deserved a grave:

And on that eve had gone to Mosque,
And thence to feast in his Kiosk.
Such is the tale his Nubians tell,
Who did not watch their charge too well;
But others say, that on that night,
By pale Phingari's trembling light,
The Giaour upon his jet-black steed
Was seen, but seen alone to speed
With bloody spur along the shore,
Nor maid nor page behind him bore.

   Her eye's dark charm 'twere vain to tell,
But gaze on that of the Gazelle,
It will assist thy fancy well;
As large, as languishingly dark,
But Soul beamed forth in every spark
That darted from beneath the lid,
Bright as the jewel of Giamschid.
Yea, *Soul*, and should our prophet say
That form was nought but breathing clay,
By Alla! I would answer nay;
Though on Al-Sirat's arch I stood,
Which totters o'er the fiery flood,
With Paradise within my view,
And all his Houris beckoning through.
Oh! who young Leila's glance could read
And keep that portion of his creed
Which saith that woman is but dust,
A soulless toy for tyrant's lust?
On her might Muftis gaze, and own

That through her eye the Immortal shone;
On her fair cheek's unfading hue
The young pomegranate's blossoms strew
Their bloom in blushes ever new;
Her hair in hyacinthine flow,
When left to roll its folds below,
As midst her handmaids in the hall
She stood superior to them all,
Hath swept the marble where her feet
Gleamed whiter than the mountain sleet
Ere from the cloud that gave it birth
It fell, and caught one stain of earth.
The cygnet nobly walks the water;
So moved on earth Circassia's daughter,
The loveliest bird of Franguestan!
As rears her crest the ruffled Swan,
 And spurns the wave with wings of pride,
When pass the steps of stranger man
 Along the banks that bound her tide;
Thus rose fair Leila's whiter neck:—
Thus armed with beauty would she check
Intrusion's glance, till Folly's gaze
Shrunk from the charms it meant to praise.
Thus high and graceful was her gait;
Her heart as tender to her mate;
Her mate—stern Hassan, who was he?
Alas! that name was not for thee!

 Stern Hassan hath a journey ta'en
With twenty vassals in his train,

Each armed, as best becomes a man,
With arquebuss and ataghan;
The chief before, as decked for war,
Bears in his belt the scimitar
Stained with the best of Arnaut blood,
When in the pass the rebels stood,
And few returned to tell the tale
Of what befell in Parne's vale.
The pistols which his girdle bore
Were those that once a Pasha wore,
Which still, though gemmed and bossed with gold,
Even robbers tremble to behold.
'Tis said he goes to woo a bride
More true than her who left his side;
The faithless slave that broke her bower,
And—worse than faithless—for a Giaour!

...

    As rolls the river into Ocean,
In sable torrent wildly streaming;
    As the sea-tide's opposing motion,
In azure column proudly gleaming,
Beats back the current many a rood,
In curling foam and mingling flood,
While eddying whirl, and breaking wave,
Roused by the blast of winter, rave;
Through sparkling spray, in thundering clash,
The lightnings of the waters flash
In awful whiteness o'er the shore,

That shines and shakes beneath the roar;
Thus—as the stream and Ocean greet,
With waves that madden as they meet—
Thus join the bands, whom mutual wrong,
And fate, and fury, drive along.
The bickering sabres' shivering jar;
    And pealing wide or ringing near
    Its echoes on the throbbing ear,
The deathshot hissing from afar;
The shock, the shout, the groan of war,
    Reverberate along that vale,
    More suited to the shepherd's tale:
Though few the numbers—theirs the strife,
That neither spares nor speaks for life!
Ah! fondly youthful hearts can press,
To seize and share the dear caress;
But Love itself could never pant
For all that Beauty sighs to grant
With half the fervour Hate bestows
Upon the last embrace of foes,
When grappling in the fight they fold
Those arms that ne'er shall lose their hold:
Friends meet to part; Love laughs at faith;
True foes, once met, are joined till death!

    With sabre shivered to the hilt,
Yet dripping with the blood he spilt;
Yet strained within the severed hand
Which quivers round that faithless brand;
His turban far behind him rolled,

And cleft in twain its firmest fold;
His flowing robe by falchion torn,
And crimson as those clouds of morn
That, streaked with dusky red, portend
The day shall have a stormy end;
A stain on every bush that bore
A fragment of his palampore;
His breast with wounds unnumbered riven,
His back to earth, his face to Heaven,
Fall'n Hassan lies—his unclosed eye
Yet lowering on his enemy,
As if the hour that sealed his fate
Surviving left his quenchless hate;
And o'er him bends that foe with brow
As dark as his that bled below.

   "Yes, Leila sleeps beneath the wave,
But his shall be a redder grave;
Her spirit pointed well the steel
Which taught that felon heart to feel.
He called the Prophet, but his power
Was vain against the vengeful Giaour:
He called on Alla—but the word
Arose unheeded or unheard.
Thou Paynim fool! could Leila's prayer
Be passed, and thine accorded there?
I watched my time, I leagued with these,
The traitor in his turn to seize;
My wrath is wreaked, the deed is done,
And now I go—but go alone."

...

    A Turban carved in coarsest stone,
A Pillar with rank weeds o'ergrown,
Whereon can now be scarcely read
The Koran verse that mourns the dead,
Point out the spot where Hassan fell
A victim in that lonely dell.
There sleeps as true an Osmanlie
As e'er at Mecca bent the knee;
As ever scorned forbidden wine,
Or prayed with face towards the shrine,
In orisons resumed anew
At solemn sound of "Alla Hu!"
Yet died he by a stranger's hand,
And stranger in his native land;
Yet died he as in arms he stood,
And unavenged, at least in blood.
But him the maids of Paradise
    Impatient to their halls invite,
And the dark heaven of Houris' eyes
    On him shall glance for ever bright;
They come—their kerchiefs green they wave,
And welcome with a kiss the brave!
Who falls in battle 'gainst a Giaour
Is worthiest an immortal bower.

    But thou, false Infidel! shall writhe
Beneath avenging Monkir's scythe;
And from its torments 'scape alone

To wander round lost Eblis' throne;
And fire unquenched, unquenchable,
Around, within, thy heart shall dwell;
Nor ear can hear nor tongue can tell
The tortures of that inward hell!
But first, on earth as Vampire sent,
Thy corse shall from its tomb be rent:
Then ghastly haunt thy native place,
And suck the blood of all thy race;
There from thy daughter, sister, wife,
At midnight drain the stream of life;
Yet loathe the banquet which perforce
Must feed thy livid living corse:
Thy victims ere they yet expire
Shall know the demon for their sire,
As cursing thee, thou cursing them,
Thy flowers are withered on the stem.

…

"How name ye yon lone Caloyer?
   His features I have scanned before
In mine own land: 'tis many a year,
   Since, dashing by the lonely shore,
I saw him urge as fleet a steed
As ever served a horseman's need.
But once I saw that face, yet then
It was so marked with inward pain,
I could not pass it by again;
It breathes the same dark spirit now,
As death were stamped upon his brow.

"'Tis twice three years at summer tide
    Since first among our freres he came;
And here it soothes him to abide
    For some dark deed he will not name.
But never at our Vesper prayer,
Nor e'er before Confession chair
Kneels he, nor recks he when arise
Incense or anthem to the skies,
But broods within his cell alone,
His faith and race alike unknown.
The sea from Paynim land he crost,
And here ascended from the coast;
Yet seems he not of Othman race,
But only Christian in his face:
I'd judge him some stray renegade,
Repentant of the change he made,
Save that he shuns our holy shrine,
Nor tastes the sacred bread and wine.
Great largess to these walls he brought,
And thus our Abbot's favour bought;
But were I Prior, not a day
Should brook such stranger's further stay,
Or pent within our penance cell
Should doom him there for aye to dwell.
Much in his visions mutters he
Of maiden whelmed beneath the sea;
Of sabres clashing, foemen flying,
Wrongs avenged, and Moslem dying.
On cliff he hath been known to stand,
And rave as to some bloody hand

Fresh severed from its parent limb,
Invisible to all but him,
Which beckons onward to his grave,
And lures to leap into the wave."

   Dark and unearthly is the scowl
That glares beneath his dusky cowl:
The flash of that dilating eye
Reveals too much of times gone by;
Though varying, indistinct its hue,
Oft will his glance the gazer rue,
For in it lurks that nameless spell,
Which speaks, itself unspeakable,
A spirit yet unquelled and high,
That claims and keeps ascendancy;
And like the bird whose pinions quake,
But cannot fly the gazing snake,
Will others quail beneath his look,
Nor 'scape the glance they scarce can brook.
From him the half-affrighted Friar
When met alone would fain retire,
As if that eye and bitter smile
Transferred to others fear and guile:
Not oft to smile descendeth he,
And when he doth 'tis sad to see
That he but mocks at Misery.
How that pale lip will curl and quiver!
Then fix once more as if for ever;
As if his sorrow or disdain
Forbade him e'er to smile again.

Well were it so—such ghastly mirth
From joyaunce ne'er derived its birth.
But sadder still it were to trace
What once were feelings in that face:
Time hath not yet the features fixed,
But brighter traits with evil mixed;
And there are hues not always faded,
Which speak a mind not all degraded
Even by the crimes through which it waded:
The common crowd but see the gloom
Of wayward deeds, and fitting doom;
The close observer can espy
A noble soul, and lineage high:
Alas! though both bestowed in vain,
Which Grief could change, and Guilt could stain,
It was no vulgar tenement
To which such lofty gifts were lent,
And still with little less than dread
On such the sight is riveted.
The roofless cot, decayed and rent,
    Will scarce delay the passer-by;
The tower by war or tempest bent,
While yet may frown one battlement,
    Demands and daunts the stranger's eye;
Each ivied arch, and pillar lone,
Pleads haughtily for glories gone!

"His floating robe around him folding,
    Slow sweeps he through the columned aisle;
With dread beheld, with gloom beholding

   The rites that sanctify the pile.
But when the anthem shakes the choir,
And kneel the monks, his steps retire;
By yonder lone and wavering torch
His aspect glares within the porch;
There will he pause till all is done—
And hear the prayer, but utter none.
See—by the half-illumined wall
His hood fly back, his dark hair fall,
That pale brow wildly wreathing round,
As if the Gorgon there had bound
The sablest of the serpent-braid
That o'er her fearful forehead strayed:
For he declines the convent oath,
And leaves those locks unhallowed growth,
But wears our garb in all beside;
And, not from piety but pride,
Gives wealth to walls that never heard
Of his one holy vow nor word.
Lo!—mark ye, as the harmony
Peals louder praises to the sky,
That livid cheek, that stony air
Of mixed defiance and despair!
Saint Francis, keep him from the shrine!
Else may we dread the wrath divine
Made manifest by awful sign.
If ever evil angel bore
The form of mortal, such he wore;
By all my hope of sins forgiven,
Such looks are not of earth nor heaven!"

...

    If solitude succeed to grief,
Release from pain is slight relief;
The vacant bosom's wilderness
Might thank the pang that made it less.
We loathe what none are left to share:
Even bliss—'twere woe alone to bear;
The heart once left thus desolate
Must fly at last for ease—to hate.
It is as if the dead could feel
The icy worm around them steal,
And shudder, as the reptiles creep
To revel o'er their rotting sleep,
Without the power to scare away
The cold consumers of their clay!
It is as if the desert bird,
    Whose beak unlocks her bosom's stream
    To still her famished nestlings' scream,
Nor mourns a life to them transferred,
Should rend her rash devoted breast,
And find them flown her empty nest.
The keenest pangs the wretched find
    Are rapture to the dreary void,
The leafless desert of the mind,
    The waste of feelings unemployed.
Who would be doomed to gaze upon
A sky without a cloud or sun?
Less hideous far the tempest's roar,
Than ne'er to brave the billows more—

Thrown, when the war of winds is o'er,
A lonely wreck on Fortune's shore,
'Mid sullen calm, and silent bay,
Unseen to drop by dull decay;—
Better to sink beneath the shock
Than moulder piecemeal on the rock!

  "Father! thy days have passed in peace,
    'Mid counted beads, and countless prayer;
To bid the sins of others cease,
    Thyself without a crime or care,
Save transient ills that all must bear,
Has been thy lot from youth to age;
And thou wilt bless thee from the rage
Of passions fierce and uncontrolled,
Such as thy penitents unfold,
Whose secret sins and sorrows rest
Within thy pure and pitying breast.
My days, though few, have passed below
In much of Joy, but more of Woe;
Yet still in hours of love or strife,
I've 'scaped the weariness of Life:
Now leagued with friends, now girt by foes,
I loathed the languor of repose.
Now nothing left to love or hate,
No more with hope or pride elate,
I'd rather be the thing that crawls
Most noxious o'er a dungeon's walls,
Than pass my dull, unvarying days,
Condemned to meditate and gaze.

Yet, lurks a wish within my breast
For rest—but not to feel 'tis rest.
Soon shall my Fate that wish fulfil;
    And I shall sleep without the dream
Of what I was, and would be still
    Dark as to thee my deeds may seem:
My memory now is but the tomb
Of joys long dead; my hope, their doom:
Though better to have died with those
Than bear a life of lingering woes.
My spirit shrunk not to sustain
The searching throes of ceaseless pain;
Nor sought the self-accorded grave
Of ancient fool and modern knave:
Yet death I have not feared to meet;
And in the field it had been sweet,
Had Danger wooed me on to move
The slave of Glory, not of Love.
I've braved it—not for Honour's boast;
I smile at laurels won or lost;
To such let others carve their way,
For high renown, or hireling pay:
But place again before my eyes
Aught that I deem a worthy prize—
The maid I love, the man I hate—
And I will hunt the steps of fate,
To save or slay, as these require,
Through rending steel, and rolling fire:
Nor needst thou doubt this speech from one
Who would but do—what he *hath* done.

Death is but what the haughty brave,
The weak must bear, the wretch must crave;
Then let life go to Him who gave:
I have not quailed to Danger's brow
When high and happy—need I *now*?

"I loved her, Friar! nay, adored—
　But these are words that all can use—
I proved it more in deed than word;
There's blood upon that dinted sword,
　A stain its steel can never lose:
'Twas shed for her, who died for me,
　It warmed the heart of one abhorred:
Nay, start not—no—nor bend thy knee,
　Nor midst my sins such act record;
Thou wilt absolve me from the deed,
For he was hostile to thy creed!
The very name of Nazarene
Was wormwood to his Paynim spleen.
Ungrateful fool! since but for brands
Well wielded in some hardy hands,
And wounds by Galileans given—
The surest pass to Turkish heaven—
For him his Houris still might wait
Impatient at the Prophet's gate.
I loved her—Love will find its way
Through paths where wolves would fear to prey;
And if it dares enough, 'twere hard
If Passion met not some reward—
No matter how, or where, or why,

I did not vainly seek, nor sigh:
Yet sometimes, with remorse, in vain
I wish she had not loved again.
She died—I dare not tell thee how;
But look—'tis written on my brow!
There read of Cain the curse and crime,
In characters unworn by Time:
Still, ere thou dost condemn me, pause;
Not mine the act, though I the cause.
Yet did he but what I had done
Had she been false to more than one.
Faithless to him—he gave the blow;
But true to me—I laid him low:
Howe'er deserved her doom might be,
Her treachery was truth to me;
To me she gave her heart, that all
Which Tyranny can ne'er enthrall;
And I, alas! too late to save!
Yet all I then could give, I gave—
'Twas some relief—our foe a grave.
His death sits lightly; but her fate
Has made me—what thou well mayst hate.

...

"The cold in clime are cold in blood,
Their love can scarce deserve the name;
But mine was like the lava flood
    That boils in Ætna's breast of flame.
I cannot prate in puling strain

Of Ladye-love, and Beauty's chain:
If changing cheek, and scorching vein,
Lips taught to writhe, but not complain,
If bursting heart, and maddening brain,
And daring deed, and vengeful steel,
And all that I have felt, and feel,
Betoken love—that love was mine,
And shown by many a bitter sign.
'Tis true, I could not whine nor sigh,
I knew but to obtain or die.
I die—but first I have possessed,
And come what may, I *have been* blessed.
Shall I the doom I sought upbraid?
No—reft of all, yet undismayed
But for the thought of Leila slain,
Give me the pleasure with the pain,
So would I live and love again.
I grieve, but not, my holy Guide!
For him who dies, but her who died:
She sleeps beneath the wandering wave—
Ah! had she but an earthly grave,
This breaking heart and throbbing head
Should seek and share her narrow bed.
She was a form of Life and Light,
That, seen, became a part of sight;
And rose, where'er I turned mine eye,
The Morning-star of Memory!

"Yes, Love indeed is light from heaven;
   A spark of that immortal fire

With angels shared, by Alla given,
    To lift from earth our low desire.
Devotion wafts the mind above,
But Heaven itself descends in Love;
A feeling from the Godhead caught,
To wean from self each sordid thought;
A ray of Him who formed the whole;
A Glory circling round the soul!
I grant *my* love imperfect, all
That mortals by the name miscall;
Then deem it evil, what thou wilt;
But say, oh say, *hers* was not Guilt!
She was my Life's unerring Light:
That quenched—what beam shall break my night?
Oh! would it shone to lead me still,
Although to death or deadliest ill!
Why marvel ye, if they who lose
    This present joy, this future hope,
    No more with Sorrow meekly cope;
In phrensy then their fate accuse;
In madness do those fearful deeds
    That seem to add but Guilt to Woe?
Alas! the breast that inly bleeds
    Hath nought to dread from outward blow:
Who falls from all he knows of bliss,
Cares little into what abyss.
Fierce as the gloomy vulture's now
    To thee, old man, my deeds appear:
I read abhorrence on thy brow,
    And this too was I born to bear!

'Tis true, that, like that bird of prey,
With havock have I marked my way:
But this was taught me by the dove,
To die—and know no second love.
This lesson yet hath man to learn,
Taught by the thing he dares to spurn:
The bird that sings within the brake,
The swan that swims upon the lake,
One mate, and one alone, will take.
And let the fool still prone to range,
And sneer on all who cannot change,
Partake his jest with boasting boys;
I envy not his varied joys,
But deem such feeble, heartless man,
Less than yon solitary swan;
Far, far beneath the shallow maid
He left believing and betrayed.
Such shame at least was never mine—
Leila! each thought was only thine!
My good, my guilt, my weal, my woe,
My hope on high—my all below.
Earth holds no other like to thee,
Or, if it doth, in vain for me:
For worlds I dare not view the dame
Resembling thee, yet not the same.
The very crimes that mar my youth,
This bed of death—attest my truth!
'Tis all too late—thou wert, thou art
The cherished madness of my heart!

"And she was lost—and yet I breathed,
    But not the breath of human life:
A serpent round my heart was wreathed,
    And stung my every thought to strife.
Alike all time, abhorred all place,
Shuddering I shrank from Nature's face,
Where every hue that charmed before
The blackness of my bosom wore.
The rest thou dost already know,
And all my sins, and half my woe.
But talk no more of penitence;
Thou seest I soon shall part from hence:
And if thy holy tale were true,
The deed that's done canst *thou* undo?
Think me not thankless—but this grief
Looks not to priesthood for relief.
My soul's estate in secret guess:
But wouldst thou pity more, say less.
When thou canst bid my Leila live,
Then will I sue thee to forgive;
Then plead my cause in that high place
Where purchased masses proffer grace.
Go, when the hunter's hand hath wrung
From forest-cave her shrieking young,
And calm the lonely lioness:
But soothe not—mock not *my* distress!

"In earlier days, and calmer hours,
    When heart with heart delights to blend,
Where bloom my native valley's bowers,

I had—Ah! have I now?—a friend!
To him this pledge I charge thee send,
    Memorial of a youthful vow;
I would remind him of my end:
    Though souls absorbed like mine allow
Brief thought to distant Friendship's claim,
Yet dear to him my blighted name.
'Tis strange—he prophesied my doom,
    And I have smiled—I then could smile—
When Prudence would his voice assume,
    And warn—I recked not what—the while:
But now Remembrance whispers o'er
Those accents scarcely marked before.
Say—that his bodings came to pass,
    And he will start to hear their truth,
    And wish his words had not been sooth:
Tell him—unheeding as I was,
    Through many a busy bitter scene
    Of all our golden youth had been,
In pain, my faltering tongue had tried
To bless his memory—ere I died;
But Heaven in wrath would turn away,
If Guilt should for the guiltless pray.
I do not ask him not to blame,
Too gentle he to wound my name;
And what have I to do with Fame?
I do not ask him not to mourn,
Such cold request might sound like scorn;
And what than Friendship's manly tear
May better grace a brother's bier?

But bear this ring, his own of old,
And tell him—what thou dost behold!
The withered frame, the ruined mind,
The wrack by passion left behind,
A shrivelled scroll, a scattered leaf,
Seared by the autumn blast of Grief!

   "Tell me no more of Fancy's gleam,
No, father, no, 'twas not a dream;
Alas! the dreamer first must sleep,
I only watched, and wished to weep;
But could not, for my burning brow
Throbbed to the very brain as now:
I wished but for a single tear,
As something welcome, new, and dear:
I wished it then, I wish it still;
Despair is stronger than my will.
Waste not thine orison, despair
Is mightier than thy pious prayer:
I would not, if I might, be blest;
I want no Paradise, but rest.
'Twas then—I tell thee—father! then
I saw her; yes, she lived again;
And shining in her white symar
As through yon pale gray cloud the star
Which now I gaze on, as on her,
Who looked and looks far lovelier;
Dimly I view its trembling spark;
To-morrow's night shall be more dark;
And I, before its rays appear,

That lifeless thing the living fear.
I wander—father! for my soul
Is fleeting towards the final goal.
I saw her—friar! and I rose
Forgetful of our former woes;
And rushing from my couch, I dart,
And clasp her to my desperate heart;
I clasp—what is it that I clasp?
No breathing form within my grasp,
No heart that beats reply to mine—
Yet, Leila! yet the form is thine!
And art thou, dearest, changed so much
As meet my eye, yet mock my touch?
Ah! were thy beauties e'er so cold,
I care not—so my arms enfold
The all they ever wished to hold.
Alas! around a shadow prest
They shrink upon my lonely breast;
Yet still 'tis there! In silence stands,
And beckons with beseeching hands!
With braided hair, and bright-black eye—
I knew 'twas false—she could not die!
But *he* is dead! within the dell
I saw him buried where he fell;
He comes not—for he cannot break
From earth;—why then art *thou* awake?
They told me wild waves rolled above
The face I view—the form I love;
They told me—'twas a hideous tale!—
I'd tell it, but my tongue would fail:

If true, and from thine ocean-cave
Thou com'st to claim a calmer grave,
Oh! pass thy dewy fingers o'er
This brow that then will burn no more;
Or place them on my hopeless heart:
But, Shape or Shade! whate'er thou art,
In mercy ne'er again depart!
Or farther with thee bear my soul
Than winds can waft or waters roll!

"Such is my name, and such my tale.
    Confessor! to thy secret ear
I breathe the sorrows I bewail,
    And thank thee for the generous tear
This glazing eye could never shed.
Then lay me with the humblest dead,
And, save the cross above my head,
Be neither name nor emblem spread,
By prying stranger to be read,
Or stay the passing pilgrim's tread."

He passed—nor of his name and race
Hath left a token or a trace,
Save what the Father must not say
Who shrived him on his dying day:
This broken tale was all we knew
Of her he loved, or him he slew.

Christabel

SAMUEL TAYLOR COLERIDGE　　　　　　1816

Part I

'Tis the middle of night by the castle clock,
And the owls have awakened the crowing cock;
Tu—whit! Tu—whoo!
And hark, again! the crowing cock,
How drowsily it crew.
Sir Leoline, the Baron rich,
Hath a toothless mastiff bitch;
From her kennel beneath the rock
She maketh answer to the clock,
Four for the quarters, and twelve for the hour;
Ever and aye, by shine and shower,
Sixteen short howls, not over loud;
Some say, she sees my lady's shroud.

Is the night chilly and dark?
The night is chilly, but not dark.
The thin gray cloud is spread on high,
It covers but not hides the sky.
The moon is behind, and at the full;
And yet she looks both small and dull.
The night is chill, the cloud is gray:
'Tis a month before the month of May,
And the Spring comes slowly up this way.

The lovely lady, Christabel,
Whom her father loves so well,
What makes her in the wood so late,
A furlong from the castle gate?
She had dreams all yesternight
Of her own betrothèd knight;
And she in the midnight wood will pray
For the weal of her lover that's far away.

She stole along, she nothing spoke,
The sighs she heaved were soft and low,
And naught was green upon the oak
But moss and rarest misletoe:
She kneels beneath the huge oak tree,
And in silence prayeth she.

The lady sprang up suddenly,
The lovely lady Christabel!
It moaned as near, as near can be,
But what it is she cannot tell.—
On the other side it seems to be,
Of the huge, broad-breasted, old oak tree.

The night is chill; the forest bare;
Is it the wind that moaneth bleak?
There is not wind enough in the air
To move away the ringlet curl
From the lovely lady's cheek—
There is not wind enough to twirl
The one red leaf, the last of its clan,
That dances as often as dance it can,

Hanging so light, and hanging so high,
On the topmost twig that looks up at the sky.

Hush, beating heart of Christabel!
Jesu, Maria, shield her well!
She folded her arms beneath her cloak,
And stole to the other side of the oak.
    What sees she there?

There she sees a damsel bright,
Drest in a silken robe of white,
That shadowy in the moonlight shone:
The neck that made that white robe wan,
Her stately neck, and arms were bare;
Her blue-veined feet unsandl'd were,
And wildly glittered here and there
The gems entangled in her hair.
I guess, 'twas frightful there to see
A lady so richly clad as she—
Beautiful exceedingly!

Mary mother, save me now!
(Said Christabel) And who art thou?

The lady strange made answer meet,
And her voice was faint and sweet:—
Have pity on my sore distress,
I scarce can speak for weariness:
Stretch forth thy hand, and have no fear!
Said Christabel, How camest thou here?
And the lady, whose voice was faint and sweet,
Did thus pursue her answer meet:—

My sire is of a noble line,
And my name is Geraldine:
Five warriors seized me yestermorn,
Me, even me, a maid forlorn:
They choked my cries with force and fright,
And tied me on a palfrey white.
The palfrey was as fleet as wind,
And they rode furiously behind.
They spurred amain, their steeds were white:
And once we crossed the shade of night.
As sure as Heaven shall rescue me,
I have no thought what men they be;
Nor do I know how long it is
(For I have lain entranced I wis)
Since one, the tallest of the five,
Took me from the palfrey's back,
A weary woman, scarce alive.
Some muttered words his comrades spoke:
He placed me underneath this oak;
He swore they would return with haste;
Whither they went I cannot tell—
I thought I heard, some minutes past,
Sounds as of a castle bell.
Stretch forth thy hand (thus ended she),
And help a wretched maid to flee.

Then Christabel stretched forth her hand,
And comforted fair Geraldine:
O well, bright dame! may you command
The service of Sir Leoline;

And gladly our stout chivalry
Will he send forth and friends withal
To guide and guard you safe and free
Home to your noble father's hall.

She rose: and forth with steps they passed
That strove to be, and were not, fast.
Her gracious stars the lady blest,
And thus spake on sweet Christabel:
All our household are at rest,
The hall as silent as the cell;
Sir Leoline is weak in health,
And may not well awakened be,
But we will move as if in stealth,
And I beseech your courtesy,
This night, to share your couch with me.

They crossed the moat, and Christabel
Took the key that fitted well;
A little door she opened straight,
All in the middle of the gate;
The gate that was ironed within and without,
Where an army in battle array had marched out.
The lady sank, belike through pain,
And Christabel with might and main
Lifted her up, a weary weight,
Over the threshold of the gate:
Then the lady rose again,
And moved, as she were not in pain.

So free from danger, free from fear,
They crossed the court: right glad they were.
And Christabel devoutly cried
To the lady by her side,
Praise we the Virgin all divine
Who hath rescued thee from thy distress!
Alas, alas! said Geraldine,
I cannot speak for weariness.
So free from danger, free from fear,
They crossed the court: right glad they were.

Outside her kennel, the mastiff old
Lay fast asleep, in moonshine cold.
The mastiff old did not awake,
Yet she an angry moan did make!
And what can ail the mastiff bitch?
Never till now she uttered yell
Beneath the eye of Christabel.
Perhaps it is the owlet's scritch:
For what can ail the mastiff bitch?

They passed the hall, that echoes still,
Pass as lightly as you will!
The brands were flat, the brands were dying,
Amid their own white ashes lying;
But when the lady passed, there came
A tongue of light, a fit of flame;
And Christabel saw the lady's eye,
And nothing else saw she thereby,
Save the boss of the shield of Sir Leoline tall,
Which hung in a murky old niche in the wall.

O softly tread, said Christabel,
My father seldom sleepeth well.

Sweet Christabel her feet doth bare,
And jealous of the listening air
They steal their way from stair to stair,
Now in glimmer, and now in gloom,
And now they pass the Baron's room,
As still as death, with stifled breath!
And now have reached her chamber door;
And now doth Geraldine press down
The rushes of the chamber floor.

The moon shines dim in the open air,
And not a moonbeam enters here.
But they without its light can see
The chamber carved so curiously,
Carved with figures strange and sweet,
All made out of the carver's brain,
For a lady's chamber meet:
The lamp with twofold silver chain
Is fastened to an angel's feet.

The silver lamp burns dead and dim;
But Christabel the lamp will trim.
She trimmed the lamp, and made it bright,
And left it swinging to and fro,
While Geraldine, in wretched plight,
Sank down upon the floor below.

O weary lady, Geraldine,
I pray you, drink this cordial wine!
It is a wine of virtuous powers;
My mother made it of wild flowers.

And will your mother pity me,
Who am a maiden most forlorn?
Christabel answered—Woe is me!
She died the hour that I was born.
I have heard the grey-haired friar tell
How on her death-bed she did say,
That she should hear the castle-bell
Strike twelve upon my wedding-day.
O mother dear! that thou wert here!
I would, said Geraldine, she were!

But soon with altered voice, said she—
"Off, wandering mother! Peak and pine!
I have power to bid thee flee."
Alas! what ails poor Geraldine?
Why stares she with unsettled eye?
Can she the bodiless dead espy?

And why with hollow voice cries she,
"Off, woman, off! this hour is mine—
Though thou her guardian spirit be,
Off, woman, off! 'tis given to me."

Then Christabel knelt by the lady's side,
And raised to heaven her eyes so blue—
Alas! said she, this ghastly ride—
Dear lady! it hath wildered you!

The lady wiped her moist cold brow,
And faintly said, "'Tis over now!"

Again the wild-flower wine she drank:
Her fair large eyes 'gan glitter bright,
And from the floor whereon she sank,
The lofty lady stood upright:
She was most beautiful to see,
Like a lady of a far countrèe.

And thus the lofty lady spake—
"All they who live in the upper sky,
Do love you, holy Christabel!
And you love them, and for their sake
And for the good which me befel,
Even I in my degree will try,
Fair maiden, to requite you well.
But now unrobe yourself; for I
Must pray, ere yet in bed I lie."

Quoth Christabel, So let it be!
And as the lady bade, did she.
Her gentle limbs did she undress,
And lay down in her loveliness.

But through her brain of weal and woe
So many thoughts moved to and fro,
That vain it were her lids to close;
So half-way from the bed she rose,
And on her elbow did recline
To look at the lady Geraldine.

Beneath the lamp the lady bowed,
And slowly rolled her eyes around;
Then drawing in her breath aloud,
Like one that shuddered, she unbound
The cincture from beneath her breast:
Her silken robe, and inner vest,
Dropt to her feet, and full in view,
Behold! her bosom and half her side—
A sight to dream of, not to tell!
O shield her! shield sweet Christabel!

Yet Geraldine nor speaks nor stirs;
Ah! what a stricken look was hers!
Deep from within she seems half-way
To lift some weight with sick assay,
And eyes the maid and seeks delay;
Then suddenly, as one defied,
Collects herself in scorn and pride,
And lay down by the Maiden's side!—
And in her arms the maid she took,
    Ah wel-a-day!
And with low voice and doleful look
These words did say:
"In the touch of this bosom there worketh a spell,
Which is lord of thy utterance, Christabel!
Thou knowest to-night, and wilt know to-morrow,
This mark of my shame, this seal of my sorrow;
    But vainly thou warrest,
        For this is alone in
    Thy power to declare,

    That in the dim forest
    Thou heard'st a low moaning,
And found'st a bright lady, surpassingly fair;
And didst bring her home with thee in love and in charity,
To shield her and shelter her from the damp air."

The Conclusion to Part I

It was a lovely sight to see
The lady Christabel, when she
Was praying at the old oak tree.
    Amid the jaggèd shadows
    Of mossy leafless boughs,
    Kneeling in the moonlight,
    To make her gentle vows;
Her slender palms together prest,
Heaving sometimes on her breast;
Her face resigned to bliss or bale—
Her face, oh call it fair not pale,
And both blue eyes more bright than clear,
Each about to have a tear.

With open eyes (ah woe is me!)
Asleep, and dreaming fearfully,
Fearfully dreaming, yet, I wis,
Dreaming that alone, which is—
O sorrow and shame! Can this be she,
The lady, who knelt at the old oak tree?
And lo! the worker of these harms,
That holds the maiden in her arms,

Seems to slumber still and mild,
As a mother with her child.

A star hath set, a star hath risen,
O Geraldine! since arms of thine
Have been the lovely lady's prison.
O Geraldine! one hour was thine—
Thou'st had thy will! By tairn and rill,
The night-birds all that hour were still.
But now they are jubilant anew,
From cliff and tower, tu—whoo! tu—whoo!
Tu—whoo! tu—whoo! from wood and fell!

And see! the lady Christabel
Gathers herself from out her trance;
Her limbs relax, her countenance
Grows sad and soft; the smooth thin lids
Close o'er her eyes; and tears she sheds—
Large tears that leave the lashes bright!
And oft the while she seems to smile
As infants at a sudden light!

Yea, she doth smile, and she doth weep,
Like a youthful hermitess,
Beauteous in a wilderness,
Who, praying always, prays in sleep.
And, if she move unquietly,
Perchance, 'tis but the blood so free
Comes back and tingles in her feet.
No doubt, she hath a vision sweet.
What if her guardian spirit 'twere,

What if she knew her mother near?
But this she knows, in joys and woes,
That saints will aid if men will call:
For the blue sky bends over all!

Part II

Each matin bell, the Baron saith,
Knells us back to a world of death.
These words Sir Leoline first said,
When he rose and found his lady dead:
These words Sir Leoline will say
Many a morn to his dying day!

And hence the custom and law began
That still at dawn the sacristan,
Who duly pulls the heavy bell,
Five and forty beads must tell
Between each stroke—a warning knell,
Which not a soul can choose but hear
From Bratha Head to Wyndermere.

Saith Bracy the bard, So let it knell!
And let the drowsy sacristan
Still count as slowly as he can!
There is no lack of such, I ween,
As well fill up the space between.
In Langdale Pike and Witch's Lair,
And Dungeon-ghyll so foully rent,
With ropes of rock and bells of air
Three sinful sextons' ghosts are pent,

Who all give back, one after t'other,
The death-note to their living brother;
And oft too, by the knell offended,
Just as their one! two! three! is ended,
The devil mocks the doleful tale
With a merry peal from Borodale.

The air is still! through mist and cloud
That merry peal comes ringing loud;
And Geraldine shakes off her dread,
And rises lightly from the bed;
Puts on her silken vestments white,
And tricks her hair in lovely plight,
And nothing doubting of her spell
Awakens the lady Christabel.
"Sleep you, sweet lady Christabel?
I trust that you have rested well."

And Christabel awoke and spied
The same who lay down by her side—
O rather say, the same whom she
Raised up beneath the old oak tree!
Nay, fairer yet! and yet more fair!
For she belike hath drunken deep
Of all the blessedness of sleep!
And while she spake, her looks, her air
Such gentle thankfulness declare,
That (so it seemed) her girded vests
Grew tight beneath her heaving breasts.
"Sure I have sinn'd!" said Christabel,
"Now heaven be praised if all be well!"

And in low faltering tones, yet sweet,
Did she the lofty lady greet
With such perplexity of mind
As dreams too lively leave behind.

So quickly she rose, and quickly arrayed
Her maiden limbs, and having prayed
That He, who on the cross did groan,
Might wash away her sins unknown,
She forthwith led fair Geraldine
To meet her sire, Sir Leoline.

The lovely maid and the lady tall
Are pacing both into the hall,
And pacing on through page and groom,
Enter the Baron's presence-room.

The Baron rose, and while he prest
His gentle daughter to his breast,
With cheerful wonder in his eyes
The lady Geraldine espies,
And gave such welcome to the same,
As might beseem so bright a dame!

But when he heard the lady's tale,
And when she told her father's name,
Why waxed Sir Leoline so pale,
Murmuring o'er the name again,
Lord Roland de Vaux of Tryermaine?
Alas! they had been friends in youth;
But whispering tongues can poison truth;

And constancy lives in realms above;
And life is thorny; and youth is vain;
And to be wroth with one we love
Doth work like madness in the brain.
And thus it chanced, as I divine,
With Roland and Sir Leoline.
Each spake words of high disdain
And insult to his heart's best brother:
They parted—ne'er to meet again!
But never either found another
To free the hollow heart from paining—
They stood aloof, the scars remaining,
Like cliffs which had been rent asunder;
A dreary sea now flows between;—
But neither heat, nor frost, nor thunder,
Shall wholly do away, I ween,
The marks of that which once hath been.

Sir Leoline, a moment's space,
Stood gazing on the damsel's face:
And the youthful Lord of Tryermaine
Came back upon his heart again.

O then the Baron forgot his age,
His noble heart swelled high with rage;
He swore by the wounds in Jesu's side
He would proclaim it far and wide,
With trump and solemn heraldry,
That they, who thus had wronged the dame,
Were base as spotted infamy!
"And if they dare deny the same,

My herald shall appoint a week,
And let the recreant traitors seek
My tourney court—that there and then
I may dislodge their reptile souls
From the bodies and forms of men!"
He spake: his eye in lightning rolls!
For the lady was ruthlessly seized; and he kenned
In the beautiful lady the child of his friend!

And now the tears were on his face,
And fondly in his arms he took
Fair Geraldine, who met the embrace,
Prolonging it with joyous look.
Which when she viewed, a vision fell
Upon the soul of Christabel,
The vision of fear, the touch and pain!
She shrunk and shuddered, and saw again—
(Ah, woe is me! Was it for thee,
Thou gentle maid! such sights to see?)

Again she saw that bosom old,
Again she felt that bosom cold,
And drew in her breath with a hissing sound:
Whereat the Knight turned wildly round,
And nothing saw, but his own sweet maid
With eyes upraised, as one that prayed.

The touch, the sight, had passed away,
And in its stead that vision blest,
Which comforted her after-rest
While in the lady's arms she lay,

Had put a rapture in her breast,
And on her lips and o'er her eyes
Spread smiles like light!
           With new surprise,
"What ails then my belovèd child?"
The Baron said—His daughter mild
Made answer, "All will yet be well!"
I ween, she had no power to tell
Aught else: so mighty was the spell.

Yet he, who saw this Geraldine,
Had deemed her sure a thing divine:
Such sorrow with such grace she blended,
As if she feared she had offended
Sweet Christabel, that gentle maid!
And with such lowly tones she prayed
She might be sent without delay
Home to her father's mansion.
                            "Nay!
Nay, by my soul!" said Leoline.
"Ho! Bracy the bard, the charge be thine!
Go thou, with sweet music and loud,
And take two steeds with trappings proud,
And take the youth whom thou lov'st best
To bear thy harp, and learn thy song,
And clothe you both in solemn vest,
And over the mountains haste along,
Lest wandering folk, that are abroad,
Detain you on the valley road.

"And when he has crossed the Irthing flood,
My merry bard! he hastes, he hastes
Up Knorren Moor, through Halegarth Wood,
And reaches soon that castle good
Which stands and threatens Scotland's wastes.

"Bard Bracy! bard Bracy! your horses are fleet,
Ye must ride up the hall, your music so sweet,
More loud than your horses' echoing feet!
And loud and loud to Lord Roland call,
Thy daughter is safe in Langdale hall!
Thy beautiful daughter is safe and free—
Sir Leoline greets thee thus through me!
He bids thee come without delay
With all thy numerous array
And take thy lovely daughter home:
And he will meet thee on the way
With all his numerous array
White with their panting palfreys' foam:
And, by mine honour! I will say,
That I repent me of the day
When I spake words of fierce disdain
To Roland de Vaux of Tryermaine!—
—For since that evil hour hath flown,
Many a summer's sun hath shone;
Yet ne'er found I a friend again
Like Roland de Vaux of Tryermaine."

The lady fell, and clasped his knees,
Her face upraised, her eyes o'erflowing;
And Bracy replied, with faltering voice,

His gracious Hail on all bestowing!—
"Thy words, thou sire of Christabel,
Are sweeter than my harp can tell;
Yet might I gain a boon of thee,
This day my journey should not be,
So strange a dream hath come to me,
That I had vowed with music loud
To clear yon wood from thing unblest.
Warned by a vision in my rest!
For in my sleep I saw that dove,
That gentle bird, whom thou dost love,
And call'st by thy own daughter's name—
Sir Leoline! I saw the same
Fluttering, and uttering fearful moan,
Among the green herbs in the forest alone.
Which when I saw and when I heard,
I wonder'd what might ail the bird;
For nothing near it could I see
Save the grass and green herbs underneath the old tree.

"And in my dream methought I went
To search out what might there be found;
And what the sweet bird's trouble meant,
That thus lay fluttering on the ground.
I went and peered, and could descry
No cause for her distressful cry;
But yet for her dear lady's sake
I stooped, methought, the dove to take,
When lo! I saw a bright green snake
Coiled around its wings and neck.

Green as the herbs on which it couched,
Close by the dove's its head it crouched;
And with the dove it heaves and stirs,
Swelling its neck as she swelled hers!
I woke; it was the midnight hour,
The clock was echoing in the tower;
But though my slumber was gone by,
This dream it would not pass away—
It seems to live upon my eye!

And thence I vowed this self-same day
With music strong and saintly song
To wander through the forest bare,
Lest aught unholy loiter there."

Thus Bracy said: the Baron, the while,
Half-listening heard him with a smile;
Then turned to Lady Geraldine,
His eyes made up of wonder and love;
And said in courtly accents fine,
"Sweet maid, Lord Roland's beauteous dove,
With arms more strong than harp or song,
Thy sire and I will crush the snake!"
He kissed her forehead as he spake,
And Geraldine in maiden wise
Casting down her large bright eyes,
With blushing cheek and courtesy fine
She turned her from Sir Leoline;
Softly gathering up her train,
That o'er her right arm fell again;

And folded her arms across her chest,
And couched her head upon her breast,
And looked askance at Christabel
Jesu, Maria, shield her well!

A snake's small eye blinks dull and shy;
And the lady's eyes they shrunk in her head,
Each shrunk up to a serpent's eye
And with somewhat of malice, and more of dread,
At Christabel she looked askance!—
One moment—and the sight was fled!
But Christabel in dizzy trance
Stumbling on the unsteady ground
Shuddered aloud, with a hissing sound;
And Geraldine again turned round,
And like a thing, that sought relief,
Full of wonder and full of grief,
She rolled her large bright eyes divine
Wildly on Sir Leoline.

The maid, alas! her thoughts are gone,
She nothing sees—no sight but one!
The maid, devoid of guile and sin,
I know not how, in fearful wise,
So deeply she had drunken in
That look, those shrunken serpent eyes,
That all her features were resigned
To this sole image in her mind:
And passively did imitate
That look of dull and treacherous hate!

And thus she stood, in dizzy trance;
Still picturing that look askance
With forced unconscious sympathy
Full before her father's view—
As far as such a look could be
In eyes so innocent and blue!

And when the trance was o'er, the maid
Paused awhile, and inly prayed:
Then falling at the Baron's feet,
"By my mother's soul do I entreat
That thou this woman send away!"
She said: and more she could not say:
For what she knew she could not tell,
O'er-mastered by the mighty spell.

Why is thy cheek so wan and wild,
Sir Leoline? Thy only child
Lies at thy feet, thy joy, thy pride,
So fair, so innocent, so mild;
The same, for whom thy lady died!
O by the pangs of her dear mother
Think thou no evil of thy child!
For her, and thee, and for no other,
She prayed the moment ere she died:
Prayed that the babe for whom she died,
Might prove her dear lord's joy and pride!
    That prayer her deadly pangs beguiled,
        Sir Leoline!
    And wouldst thou wrong thy only child,
        Her child and thine?

Within the Baron's heart and brain
If thoughts, like these, had any share,
They only swelled his rage and pain,
And did but work confusion there.
His heart was cleft with pain and rage,
His cheeks they quivered, his eyes were wild,
Dishonoured thus in his old age;
Dishonoured by his only child,
And all his hospitality
To the wronged daughter of his friend
By more than woman's jealousy
Brought thus to a disgraceful end—
He rolled his eye with stern regard
Upon the gentle minstrel bard,
And said in tones abrupt, austere—
"Why, Bracy! dost thou loiter here?
I bade thee hence!" The bard obeyed;
And turning from his own sweet maid,
The agèd knight, Sir Leoline,
Led forth the lady Geraldine!

The Conclusion to Part II

A little child, a limber elf,
Singing, dancing to itself,
A fairy thing with red round cheeks,
That always finds, and never seeks,
Makes such a vision to the sight
As fills a father's eyes with light;
And pleasures flow in so thick and fast

Upon his heart, that he at last
Must needs express his love's excess
With words of unmeant bitterness.
Perhaps 'tis pretty to force together
Thoughts so all unlike each other;
To mutter and mock a broken charm,
To dally with wrong that does no harm.
Perhaps 'tis tender too and pretty
At each wild word to feel within
A sweet recoil of love and pity.
And what, if in a world of sin
(O sorrow and shame should this be true!)
Such giddiness of heart and brain
Comes seldom save from rage and pain,
So talks as it's most used to do.

From *Maud*

ALFRED, LORD TENNYSON 1855

Part I

I.

1.

I hate the dreadful hollow behind the little wood,
Its lips in the field above are dabbled with blood-red
    heath,
The red-ribb'd ledges drip with a silent horror of blood,
And Echo there, whatever is ask'd her, answers "Death."

2.

For there in the ghastly pit long since a body was found,
His who had given me life—O father! O God! was it
    well?—
Mangled, and flatten'd, and crush'd, and dinted into the
    ground:
There yet lies the rock that fell with him when he fell.

3.

Did he fling himself down? who knows? for a vast
    speculation had fail'd,
And ever he mutter'd and madden'd, and ever wann'd
    with despair,

And out he walk'd when the wind like a broken worldling wail'd,
And the flying gold of the ruin'd woodlands drove thro' the air.

4.

I remember the time, for the roots of my hair were stirr'd
By a shuffled step, by a dead weight trail'd, by a whisper'd fright,
And my pulses closed their gates with a shock on my heart as I heard
The shrill-edged shriek of a mother divide the shuddering night.

5.

Villainy somewhere! whose? One says, we are villains all.
Not he: his honest fame should at least by me be maintained:
But that old man, now lord of the broad estate and the Hall,
Dropt off gorged from a scheme that had left us flaccid and drain'd.

6.

Why do they prate of the blessings of Peace? we have made them a curse,
Pickpockets, each hand lusting for all that is not its own;
And lust of gain, in the spirit of Cain, is it better or worse
Than the heart of the citizen hissing in war on his own hearthstone?

7.

But these are the days of advance, the works of the men of mind,
When who but a fool would have faith in a tradesman's ware or his word?
Is it peace or war? Civil war, as I think, and that of a kind
The viler, as underhand, not openly bearing the sword.

8.

Sooner or later I too may passively take the print
Of the golden age—why not? I have neither hope nor trust;
May make my heart as a millstone, set my face as a flint,
Cheat and be cheated, and die: who knows? we are ashes and dust.

9.

Peace sitting under her olive, and slurring the days gone by,
When the poor are hovell'd and hustled together, each sex, like swine,
When only the ledger lives, and when only not all men lie;
Peace in her vineyard—yes!?—but a company forges the wine.

10.

And the vitriol madness flushes up in the ruffian's head,
Till the filthy by-lane rings to the yell of the trampled wife,

While chalk and alum and plaster are sold to the poor for bread,
And the spirit of murder works in the very means of life.

11.

And Sleep must lie down arm'd, for the villainous centre-bits
Grind on the wakeful ear in the hush of the moonless nights,
While another is cheating the sick of a few last gasps, as he sits
To pestle a poison'd poison behind his crimson lights.

12.

When a Mammonite mother kills her babe for a burial fee,
And Timour-Mammon grins on a pile of children's bones,
Is it peace or war? better, war! loud war by land and by sea,
War with a thousand battles, and shaking a hundred thrones.

13.

For I trust if an enemy's fleet came yonder round by the hill,
And the rushing battle-bolt sang from the three-decker out of the foam,
That the smoothfaced snubnosed rogue would leap from his counter and till,
And strike, if he could, were it but with his cheating yardwand, home.———

14.

What! am I raging alone as my father raged in his mood?
Must *I* too creep to the hollow and dash myself down and die
Rather than hold by the law that I made, nevermore to brood
On a horror of shatter'd limbs and a wretched swindler's lie?

15.

Would there be sorrow for *me*? there was *love* in the passionate shriek,
Love for the silent thing that had made false haste to the grave—
Wrapt in a cloak, as I saw him, and thought he would rise and speak
And rave at the lie and the liar, ah God, as he used to rave.

16.

I am sick of the Hall and the hill, I am sick of the moor and the main.
Why should I stay? can a sweeter chance ever come to me here?
O, having the nerves of motion as well as the nerves of pain,
Were it not wise if I fled from the place and the pit and the fear?

17.

There are workmen up at the Hall: they are coming back
    from abroad;
The dark old place will be gilt by the touch of a
    millionnaire:
I have heard, I know not whence, of the singular beauty of
    Maud;
I play'd with the girl when a child; she promised then to be
    fair.

18.

Maud with her venturous climbings and tumbles and
    childish escapes,
Maud the delight of the village, the ringing joy of the Hall,
Maud with her sweet purse-mouth when my father
    dangled the grapes,
Maud the beloved of my mother, the moon-faced darling
    of all,—

19.

What is she now? My dreams are bad. She may bring me a
    curse.
No, there is fatter game on the moor; she will let me alone.
Thanks, for the fiend best knows whether woman or man
    be the worse.
I will bury myself in my books, and the Devil may pipe to
    his own.

II.

Long have I sigh'd for a calm: God grant I may find it at last!
It will never be broken by Maud, she has neither savour nor salt,
But a cold and clear-cut face, as I found when her carriage past,
Perfectly beautiful: let it be granted her: where is the fault?
All that I saw (for her eyes were downcast, not to be seen)
Faultily faultless, icily regular, splendidly null,
Dead perfection, no more; nothing more, if it had not been
For a chance of travel, a paleness, an hour's defect of the rose,
Or an underlip, you may call it a little too ripe, too full,
Or the least little delicate aquiline curve in a sensitive nose,
From which I escaped heart-free, with the least little touch of spleen.

III.

Cold and clear-cut face, why come you so cruelly meek,
Breaking a slumber in which all spleenful folly was drown'd,
Pale with the golden beam of an eyelash dead on the cheek,
Passionless, pale, cold face, star-sweet on a gloom profound;
Womanlike, taking revenge too deep for a transient wrong

Done but in thought to your beauty, and ever as pale as before
Growing and fading and growing upon me without a sound.
Luminous, gemlike, ghostlike, deathlike, half the night long
Growing and fading and growing, till I could bear it no
    more.
But arose, and all by myself in my own dark garden ground,
Listening now to the tide in its broad-flung shipwrecking roar,
Now to the scream of a madden'd beach dragg'd down by
    the wave,
Walk'd in a wintry wind by a ghastly glimmer, and found
The shining daffodil dead, and Orion low in his grave.

…

XXII.

1.

Come into the garden, Maud,
    For the black bat, night, has flown,
Come into the garden, Maud,
    I am here at the gate alone;
And the woodbine spices are wafted abroad,
    And the musk of the roses blown.

2.

For a breeze of morning moves,
    And the planet of Love is on high,
Beginning to faint in the light that she loves
    On a bed of daffodil sky,

To faint in the light of the sun she loves.
    To faint in his light, and to die.

3.

All night have the roses heard
    The flute, violin, bassoon;
All night has the casement jessamine stirr'd
    To the dangers dancing in tune;
Till a silence fell with the waking bird,
    And a hush with the setting moon.

4.

I said to the lily, "There is but one
    With whom she has heart to be gay.
When will the dancers leave her alone?
    She is weary of dance and play."
Now half to the setting moon are gone,
    And half to the rising day;
Low on the sand and loud on the stone
    The last wheel echoes away.

5.

I said to the rose, "The brief night goes
    In babble and revel and wine.
Young lord-lover, what sighs are those,
    For one that will never be thine?
But mine, but mine," so I sware to the rose,
    "For ever and ever, mine."

6.

And the soul of the rose went into my blood,
    As the music clash'd in the hall;
And long by the garden lake I stood.
    For I heard your rivulet fall
From the lake to the meadow and on to the wood,
    Our wood, that is dearer than all;

7.

From the meadow your walks have left so sweet
    That whenever a March-wind sighs
He sets the jewel-print of your feet
    In violets blue as your eyes,
To the woody hollows in which we meet
    And the valleys of Paradise.

8.

The slender acacia would not shake
    One long milk-bloom on the tree;
The white lake-blossom fell into the lake,
    As the pimpernel dozed on the lea;
But the rose was awake all night for your sake,
    Knowing your promise to me;
The lilies and roses were all awake.
    They sigh'd for the dawn and thee.

9.

Queen rose of the rosebud garden of girls,
    Come hither, the dances are done,
In gloss of satin and glimmer of pearls,
    Queen lily and rose in one;
Shine out, little head, sunning over with curls,
    To the flowers, and be their sun.

10.

There has fallen a splendid tear
    From the passion-flower at the gate.
She is coming, my dove, my dear;
    She is coming, my life, my fate;
The red rose cries, "She is near, she is near;"
    And the white rose weeps, "She is late;"
The larkspur listens, "I hear, I hear;"
    And the lily whispers, "I wait."

11.

She is coming, my own, my sweet;
    Were it ever so airy a tread.
My heart would hear her and beat,
    Were it earth in an earthy bed;
My dust would hear her and beat,
    Had I lain for a century dead;
Would start and tremble under her feet,
    And blossom in purple and red.

. . .

Part II

IV.

1.

O that 'twere possible
After long grief and pain
To find the arms of my true love
Round me once again!

2.

When I was wont to meet her
In the silent woody places
By the home that gave me birth,
We stood tranced in long embraces
Mixt with kisses sweeter sweeter
Than any thing on earth.

3.

A shadow flits before me,
Not thou, but like to thee;
Ah Christ, that it were possible
For one short hour to see
The souls we loved, that they might tell us
What and where they be.

4.

It leads me forth at evening,
It lightly winds and steals

In a cold white robe before me,
When all my spirit reels
At the shouts, the leagues of lights,
And the roaring of the wheels.

5.

Half the night I waste in sighs,
Half in dreams I sorrow after
The delight of early skies;
In a wakeful doze I sorrow
For the hand, the lips, the eyes,
For the meeting of the morrow,
The delight of happy laughter,
The delight of low replies.

6.

'Tis a morning pure and sweet,
And a dewy splendour falls
On the little flower that clings
To the turrets and the walls;
'Tis a morning pure and sweet,
And the light and shadow fleet;
She is walking in the meadow,
And the woodland echo rings;
In a moment we shall meet;
She is singing in the meadow,
And the rivulet at her feet
Ripples on in light and shadow
To the ballad that she sings.

7.

Do I hear her sing as of old,
My bird with the shining head,
My own dove with the tender eye?
But there rings on a sudden a passionate cry,
There is some one dying or dead,
And a sullen thunder is roll'd;
For a tumult shakes the city,
And I wake, my dream is fled;
In the shuddering dawn, behold,
Without knowledge, without pity,
By the curtains of my bed
That abiding phantom cold.

8.

Get thee hence, nor come again,
Mix not memory with doubt,
Pass, thou deathlike type of pain,
Pass and cease to move about,
'Tis the blot upon the brain
That *will* show itself without.

9.

Then I rise, the eavedrops fall,
And the yellow vapours choke
The great city sounding wide;
The day comes, a dull red ball
Wrapt in drifts of lurid smoke
On the misty river-tide.

10.

Thro' the hubbub of the market
I steal, a wasted frame,
It crosses here, it crosses there,
Thro' all that crowd confused and loud,
The shadow still the same;
And on my heavy eyelids
My anguish hangs like shame.

11.

Alas for her that met me,
That heard me softly call,
Came glimmering thro' the laurels
At the quiet evenfall,
In the garden by the turrets
Of the old manorial hall.

12.

Would the happy spirit descend,
From the realms of light and song,
In the chamber or the street,
As she looks among the blest,
Should I fear to greet my friend
Or to say "forgive the wrong,"
Or to ask her, "take me, sweet,
To the regions of thy rest?"

13.

But the broad light glares and beats,
And the shadow flits and fleets
And will not let me be;
And I loathe the squares and streets,
And the faces that one meets,
Hearts with no love for me:
Always I long to creep
Into some still cavern deep,
There to weep, and weep, and weep
My whole soul out to thee.

V.

1.

Dead, long dead,
Long dead!
And my heart is a handful of dust,
And the wheels go over my head,
And my bones are shaken with pain,
For into a shallow grave they are thrust,
Only a yard beneath the street,
And the hoofs of the horses beat, beat,
The hoofs of the horses beat,
Beat into my scalp and my brain,
With never an end to the stream of passing feet,
Driving, hurrying, marrying, burying,
Clamour and rumble, and ringing and clatter,

And here beneath it is all as bad,
For I thought the dead had peace, but it is not so;
To have no peace in the grave, is that not sad?
But up and down and to and fro,
Ever about me the dead men go;
And then to hear a dead man chatter
Is enough to drive one mad.

2.

Wretchedest age, since Time began,
They cannot even bury a man;
And tho' we paid our tithes in the days that are gone,
Not a bell was rung, not a prayer was read;
It is that which makes us loud in the world of the dead;
There is none that does his work, not one;
A touch of their office might have sufficed,
But the churchmen fain would kill their church,
As the churches have kill'd their Christ.

3.

See, there is one of us sobbing,
No limit to his distress;
And another, a lord of all things, praying
To his own great self, as I guess;
And another, a statesman there, betraying
His party-secret, fool, to the press;
And yonder a vile physician, blabbing
The case of his patient— all for what?
To tickle the maggot born in an empty head,

And wheedle a world that loves him not.
For it is but a world of the dead.

4.

Nothing but idiot gabble!
For the prophecy given of old
And then not understood,
Has come to pass as foretold;
Not let any man think for the public good,
But babble, merely for babble.
For I never whisper'd a private affair
Within the hearing of cat or mouse,
No, not to myself in the closet alone,
But I heard it shouted at once from the top of the house;
Everything came to be known:
Who told *him* we were there?

5.

Not that gray old wolf, for he came not back
From the wilderness, full of wolves, where he used to lie;
He has gather'd the bones for his o'ergrown whelp to crack;
Crack them now for yourself, and howl, and die.

6.

Prophet, curse me the blabbing lip,
And curse me the British vermin, the rat;
I know not whether he came in the Hanover ship,
But I know that he lies and listens mute
In an ancient mansion's crannies and holes:

Arsenic, arsenic, sure, would do it.
Except that now we poison our babes, poor souls!
It is all used up for that.

7.

Tell him now: she is standing here at my head;
Not beautiful now, not even kind;
He may take her now; for she never speaks her mind,
But is ever the one thing silent here.
She is not of us, as I divine;
She comes from another stiller world of the dead,
Stiller, not fairer than mine.

8.

But I know where a garden grows,
Fairer than aught in the world beside,
All made up of the lily and rose
That blow by night, when the season is good,
To the sound of dancing music and flutes:
It is only flowers, they had no fruits,
And I almost fear they are not roses, but blood;
For the keeper was one, so full of pride,
He linkt a dead man there to a spectral bride;
For he, if he had not been a Sultan of brutes,
Would he have that hole in his side?

9.

But what will the old man say?
He laid a cruel snare in a pit

To catch a friend of mine one stormy day;
Yet now I could even weep to think of it;
For what will the old man say
When he comes to the second corpse in the pit?

10.

Friend, to be struck by the public foe,
Then to strike him and lay him low,
That were a public merit, far,
Whatever the Quaker holds, from sin;
But the red life spilt for a private blow—
I swear to you, lawful and lawless war
Are scarcely even akin.

11.

O me, why have they not buried me deep enough?
Is it kind to have made me a grave so rough,
Me, that was never a quiet sleeper?
Maybe still I am but half-dead;
Then I cannot be wholly dumb;
I will cry to the steps above my head,
And somebody, surely, some kind heart will come
To bury me, bury me
Deeper, ever so little deeper.

The Distant Moon

RAFAEL CAMPO　　　　　　　　　　　　　　　　1994

I

Admitted to the hospital again.
The second bout of pneumocystis back
In January almost killed him; then,
He'd sworn to us he'd die at home. He baked
Us cookies, which the student wouldn't eat,
Before he left—the kitchen on 5A
Is small, but serviceable and neat.
He told me stories: Richard Gere was gay
And sleeping with a friend of his, and AIDS
Was an elaborate conspiracy
Effected by the government. He stayed
Four months. He lost his sight to CMV.

II

One day, I drew his blood, and while I did
He laughed, and said I was his girlfriend now,
His blood-brother. "Vampire-slut," he cried,
"You'll make me live forever!" Wrinkled brows
Were all I managed in reply. I know
I'm drowning in his blood, his purple blood.
I filled my seven tubes; the warmth was slow

To leave them, pressed inside my palm. I'm sad
Because he doesn't see my face. Because
I can't identify with him. I hate
The fact that he's my age, and that across
My skin he's there, my blood-brother, my mate.

III

He said I was too nice, and after all
If Jodie Foster was a lesbian,
Then doctors could be queer. Residual
Guilts tingled down my spine. "OK, I'm done,"
I said as I withdrew the needle from
His back, and pressed. The CSF was clear;
I never answered him. That spot was framed
In sterile, paper drapes. He was so near
Death, telling him seemed pointless. Then, he died.
Unrecognizable to anyone
But me, he left my needles deep inside
His joking heart. An autopsy was done.

IV

I'd read to him at night. His horoscope,
The New York Times, The Advocate;
Some lines by Richard Howard gave us hope.
A quiet hospital is infinite,
The polished, ice-white floors, the darkened halls
That lead to almost anywhere, to death

Or ghostly, lighted Coke machines. I call
To him one night, at home, asleep. His breath,
I dreamed, had filled my lungs—his lips, my lips
Had touched. I felt as though I'd touched a shrine.
Not disrespectfully, but in some lapse
Of concentration. In a mirror shines

The distant moon.

Dire Warnings

The Vampire

HEINRICH AUGUST OSSENFELDER   1748

Anonymous translation

My dear young maiden clingeth
Unbending, fast and firm
To all the long-held teaching
Of a mother ever true;
As in vampires unmortal
Folk on the Theyse's portal
Heyduck-like do believe.
But my Christine thou dost dally,
And wilt my loving parry
Till I myself avenging
To a vampire's health a-drinking
Him toast in pale tockay.

And as softly thou art sleeping
To thee shall I come creeping
And thy life's blood drain away.
And so shalt thou be trembling
For thus shall I be kissing
And death's threshold thou' it be crossing
With fear, in my cold arms.
And last shall I thee question
Compared to such instruction
What are a mother's charms?

La Belle Dame Sans Merci

JOHN KEATS   1820

O what can ail thee, knight-at-arms,
   Alone and palely loitering?
The sedge has withered from the lake,
   And no birds sing.

O what can ail thee, knight-at-arms,
   So haggard and so woe-begone?
The squirrel's granary is full,
   And the harvest's done.

I see a lily on thy brow,
   With anguish moist and fever-dew,
And on thy cheeks a fading rose
   Fast withereth too.

I met a lady in the meads,
   Full beautiful—a faery's child,
Her hair was long, her foot was light,
   And her eyes were wild.

I made a garland for her head,
   And bracelets too, and fragrant zone;
She looked at me as she did love,
   And made sweet moan

I set her on my pacing steed,
   And nothing else saw all day long,

For sidelong would she bend, and sing
    A faery's song.

She found me roots of relish sweet,
    And honey wild, and manna-dew,
And sure in language strange she said—
    "I love thee true".

She took me to her Elfin grot,
    And there she wept and sighed full sore,
And there I shut her wild wild eyes
    With kisses four.

And there she lullèd me asleep,
    And there I dreamed—Ah! woe betide!—
The latest dream I ever dreamt
    On the cold hill side.

I saw pale kings and princes too,
    Pale warriors, death-pale were they all;
They cried—"La Belle Dame sans Merci
    Thee hath in thrall!"

I saw their starved lips in the gloom,
    With horrid warning gapèd wide,
And I awoke and found me here,
    On the cold hill's side.

And this is why I sojourn here,
    Alone and palely loitering,
Though the sedge is withered from the lake,
    And no birds sing.

The Vampire Bride

HENRY THOMAS LIDDELL　　　　　　　　　　1833

"I am come—I am come! once again from the tomb,
　　In return for the ring which you gave;
That I am thine, and that thou art mine,
　　This nuptial pledge receive."

He lay like a corse 'neath the Demon's force,
　　And she wrapp'd him in a shroud;
And she fixed her teeth his heart beneath,
　　And she drank of the warm life-blood!

And ever and anon murmur'd the lips of stone,
　　"Soft and warm is this couch of thine,
Thou'lt to-morrow be laid on a colder bed—
　　Albert! that bed will be mine!"

The Vampyre

JAMES CLERK MAXWELL   1845

Thair is a knichte rydis through the wood,
And a doughty knichte is hee,
And sure hee is on a message sent,
He rydis see hastilie.
Hee passit the aik, and hee passit the birk,
And hee passit monie a tre,
Bot plesant to him was the saugh sae slim,
For beneath it hee did see
The boniest ladye that ever he saw,
Scho was see schyn and fair.
And there scho sat, beneath the saugh,
Kaiming hir gowden hair.
And then the knichte—"Oh ladye brichte,
What chance hes brought you here,
But say the word, and ye schall gang
Back to your kindred dear."
Then up and spok the Ladye fair—
"I have nae friends or kin,
Bot in a littel boat I live,
Amidst the waves' loud din."
Then answered thus the douchty knichte—
"I'll follow you through all,
For gin ye bee in a littel boat,
The world to it seemis small."

They gaed through the wood, and through the wood
To the end of the wood they came:
And when they came to the end of the wood
They saw the salt sea faem.
And then they saw the wee, wee boat,
That daunced on the top of the wave,
And first got in the ladye fair,
And then the knichte sae brave;
They got into the wee, wee boat,
And rowed wi' a' their micht;
When the knichte sae brave, he turnit about,
And lookit at the ladye bricht;
He lookit at her bonie cheik,
And hee lookit at hir twa bricht eyne,
Bot hir rosie cheik growe ghaistly pale,
And scho seymit as scho deid had been.
The fause fause knichte growe pale wi frichte,
And his hair rose up on end,
For gane-by days cam to his mynde,
And his former luve he kenned.
Then spake the ladye,—"Thou, fause knichte,
Hast done to mee much ill,
Thou didst forsake me long ago,
Bot I am constant still;
For though I ligg in the woods sae cald,
At rest I canna bee
Until I sucke the gude lyfe blude
Of the man that gart me dee."
Hee saw hir lipps were wet wi' blude,
And hee saw hir lyfelesse eyne,

And loud hee cry'd, "Get frae my syde,
Thou vampyr corps uncleane!"
Bot no, hee is in hir magic boat,
And on the wyde wyde sea;
And the vampyr suckis his gude lyfe blude,
Sho suckis hym till hee dee.
So now beware, whoe're you are,
That walkis in this lone wood;
Beware of that deceitfull spright,
The ghaist that suckle the blude.

Metamorphoses of the Vampire

CHARLES BAUDELAIRE 1857

Translated by George Dillon and Edna St Vincent Millay

Meanwhile from her red mouth the woman, in husky tones,
Twisting her body like a serpent upon hot stones
And straining her white breasts from their imprisonment,
Let fall these words, as potent as a heavy scent:
"My lips are moist and yielding, and I know the way
To keep the antique demon of remorse at bay.
All sorrows die upon my bosom. I can make
Old men laugh happily as children for my sake.
For him who sees me naked in my tresses, I
Replace the sun, the moon, and all the stars of the sky!
Believe me, learnèd sir, I am so deeply skilled
That when I wind a lover in my soft arms, and yield
My breasts like two ripe fruits for his devouring—both
Shy and voluptuous, insatiable and loath—
Upon this bed that groans and sighs luxuriously
Even the impotent angels would be damned for me!"

When she had drained me of my very marrow, and cold
And weak, I turned to give her one more kiss—behold,
There at my side was nothing but a hideous
Putrescent thing, all faceless and exuding pus.
I closed my eyes and mercifully swooned till day:

And when I looked at morning for that beast of prey
Who seemed to have replenished her arteries from my own,
The wan, disjointed fragments of a skeleton
Wagged up and down in a lewd posture where she had lain,
Rattling with each convulsion like a weathervane
Or an old sign that creaks upon its bracket, right
Mournfully in the wind upon a winter's night.

A Daughter of Eve

CHRISTINA ROSSETTI   1876

A fool I was to sleep at noon,
And wake when night is chilly
Beneath the comfortless cold moon;
A fool to pluck my rose too soon,
A fool to snap my lily.

My garden-plot I have not kept;
Faded and all-forsaken,
I weep as I have never wept:
Oh it was summer when I slept,
It's winter now I waken.

Talk what you please of future spring
And sun-warm'd sweet to-morrow:—
Stripp'd bare of hope and everything,
No more to laugh, no more to sing,
I sit alone with sorrow.

The Vampire

MADISON JULIUS CAWEIN   1896

A lily in a twilight place?
A moonflow'r in the lonely night?—
Strange beauty of a woman's face
    Of wildflow'r-white!

The rain that hangs a star's green ray
Slim on a leaf-point's restlessness,
Is not so glimmering green and gray
    As was her dress.

I drew her dark hair from her eyes,
And in their deeps beheld a while
Such shadowy moonlight as the skies
    Of Hell may smile.

She held her mouth up redly wan,
And burning cold,—I bent and kissed
Such rosy snow as some wild dawn
    Makes of a mist.

God shall not take from me that hour,
When round my neck her white arms clung!
When 'neath my lips, like some fierce flower,
    Her white throat swung!

Or words she murmured while she leaned!
Witch-words, she holds me softly by,—
The spell that binds me to a fiend
   Until I die.

The Vampire

RUDYARD KIPLING 1897

A Fool there was and he made his prayer
(A Fool as you and I!)
To a rag and a bone and a hank of hair
(We called her the woman who did not care)
But the fool he called her his lady fair
(Even as you and I!)
A fool there was and his goods he spent
(Even as you and I!)
Honour and faith and a sure intent
(And it wasn't the least what the lady meant)
But a fool must follow his natural bent
(Even as you and I!)

Oh, the years we waste and the tears we waste
And the work of our head and hand
Belong to the woman who did not know
(And now we know that she never could know)
And did not understand!

Oh, the toil we lost and the spoil we lost
And the excellent things we planned
Belong to the woman who didn't know why
(And now we know that she never knew why)
And did not understand!

The fool was stripped to his foolish hide
(Even as you and I!)
Which she might have seen when she threw him aside
(But it isn't on record the lady tried)
So some of him lived but the most of him died
(Even as you and I!)

And it isn't the shame and it isn't the blame
That stings like a white-hot brand.
It's coming to know that she never knew why,
(Seeing, at last, she could never know why)
And never could understand!

The Vampire

CONRAD AIKEN 1914

She rose among us where we lay.
She wept, we put our work away.
She chilled our laughter, stilled our play;
And spread a silence there.
And darkness shot across the sky,
And once, and twice, we heard her cry;
And saw her lift white hands on high
And toss her troubled hair.

What shape was this who came to us,
With basilisk eyes so ominous,
With mouth so sweet, so poisonous,
And tortured hands so pale?
We saw her wavering to and fro,
Through dark and wind we saw her go;
Yet what her name was did not know;
And felt our spirits fail.

We tried to turn away; but still
Above we heard her sorrow thrill;
And those that slept, they dreamed of ill
And dreadful things:
Of skies grown red with rending flames
And shuddering hills that cracked their frames;
Of twilights foul with wings;

And skeletons dancing to a tune;
And cries of children stifled soon;
And over all a blood-red moon
A dull and nightmare size.
They woke, and sought to go their ways,
Yet everywhere they met her gaze,
Her fixed and burning eyes.

Who are you now,—we cried to her—
Spirit so strange, so sinister?
We felt dead winds above us stir;
And in the darkness heard
A voice fall, singing, cloying sweet,
Heavily dropping, though that heat,
Heavy as honeyed pulses beat,
Slow word by anguished word.

And through the night strange music went
With voice and cry so darkly blent
We could not fathom what they meant;
Save only that they seemed
To thin the blood along our veins,
Foretelling vile, delirious pains,
And clouds divulging blood-red rains
Upon a hill undreamed.

And this we heard: "Who dies for me,
He shall possess me secretly,
My terrible beauty he shall see,
And slake my body's flame.
But who denies me cursed shall be,

And slain, and buried loathsomely,
And slimed upon with shame."

And darkness fell. And like a sea
Of stumbling deaths we followed, we
Who dared not stay behind.
There all night long beneath a cloud
We rose and fell, we struck and bowed,
We were the ploughman and the ploughed,
Our eyes were red and blind.

And some, they said, had touched her side,
Before she fled us there;
And some had taken her to bride;
And some lain down for her and died;
Who had not touched her hair,
Ran to and fro and cursed and cried
And sought her everywhere.

"Her eyes have feasted on the dead,
And small and shapely is her head,
And dark and small her mouth," they said,
"And beautiful to kiss;
Her mouth is sinister and red
As blood in moonlight is."

Then poets forgot their jeweled words
And cut the sky with glittering swords;
And innocent souls turned carrion birds
To perch upon the dead.
Sweet daisy fields were drenched with death,

The air became a charnel breath,
Pale stones were splashed with red.

Green leaves were dappled bright with blood
And fruit trees murdered in the bud;
And when at length the dawn
Came green as twilight from the east,
And all that heaving horror ceased,
Silent was every bird and beast,
And that dark voice was gone.

No word was there, no song, no bell,
No furious tongue that dream to tell;
Only the dead, who rose and fell
Above the wounded men;
And whisperings and wails of pain
Blown slowly from the wounded grain,
Blown slowly from the smoking plain;
And silence fallen again.

Until at dusk, from God knows where,
Beneath dark birds that filled the air,
Like one who did not hear or care,
Under a blood-red cloud,
An aged ploughman came alone
And drove his share through flesh and bone,
And turned them under to mould and stone;
All night long he ploughed.

Witch-Wife

EDNA ST VINCENT MILLAY 1923

She is neither pink nor pale,
    And she never will be all mine;
She learned her hands in a fairy-tale,
    And her mouth on a valentine.

She has more hair than she needs;
    In the sun 'tis a woe to me!
And her voice is a string of colored beads,
    Or steps leading into the sea.

She loves me all that she can,
    And her ways to my ways resign;
But she was not made for any man,
    And she never will be all mine.

The White Witch

JAMES WELDON JOHNSON 1922

O brothers mine, take care! Take care!
The great white witch rides out to-night.
Trust not your prowess nor your strength,
Your only safety lies in flight;
For in her glance there is a snare,
And in her smile there is a blight.

The great white witch you have not seen?
Then, younger brothers mine, forsooth,
Like nursery children you have looked
For ancient hag and snaggle-tooth;
But no, not so; the witch appears
In all the glowing charms of youth.

Her lips are like carnations, red,
Her face like new-born lilies, fair,
Her eyes like ocean waters, blue,
She moves with subtle grace and air,
And all about her head there floats
The golden glory of her hair.

But though she always thus appears
In form of youth and mood of mirth,
Unnumbered centuries are hers,
The infant planets saw her birth;

The child of throbbing Life is she,
Twin sister to the greedy earth.

And back behind those smiling lips,
And down within those laughing eyes,
And underneath the soft caress
Of hand and voice and purring sighs,
The shadow of the panther lurks,
The spirit of the vampire lies.

For I have seen the great white witch,
And she has led me to her lair,
And I have kissed her red, red lips
And cruel face so white and fair;
Around me she has twined her arms,
And bound me with her yellow hair.

I felt those red lips burn and sear
My body like a living coal;
Obeyed the power of those eyes
As the needle trembles to the pole;
And did not care although I felt
The strength go ebbing from my soul.

Oh! she has seen your strong young limbs,
And heard your laughter loud and gay,
And in your voices she has caught
The echo of a far-off day,
When man was closer to the earth;
And she has marked you for her prey.

She feels the old Antaean strength
In you, the great dynamic beat
Of primal passions, and she sees
In you the last besieged retreat
Of love relentless, lusty, fierce,
Love pain-ecstatic, cruel-sweet.

O, brothers mine, take care! Take care!
The great white witch rides out to-night.
O, younger brothers mine, beware!
Look not upon her beauty bright;
For in her glance there is a snare,
And in her smile there is a blight.

The Vampire Within

To a Little Invisible Being Who is Expected Soon to Become Visible

ANNA LÆTITIA BARBAULD 1825

Germ of new life, whose powers expanding slow
For many a moon their full perfection wait,—
Haste, precious pledge of happy love, to go
Auspicious borne through life's mysterious gate.

What powers lie folded in thy curious frame,—
Senses from objects locked, and mind from thought!
How little canst thou guess thy lofty claim
To grasp at all the worlds the Almighty wrought!

And see, the genial season's warmth to share,
Fresh younglings shoot, and opening roses glow!
Swarms of new life exulting fill the air,—
Haste, infant bud of being, haste to blow!

For thee the nurse prepares her lulling songs,
The eager matrons count the lingering day;
But far the most thy anxious parent longs
On thy soft cheek a mother's kiss to lay.

She only asks to lay her burden down,
That her glad arms that burden may resume;
And nature's sharpest pangs her wishes crown,
That free thee living from thy living tomb.

She longs to fold to her maternal breast
Part of herself, yet to herself unknown;
To see and to salute the stranger guest,
Fed with her life through many a tedious moon.

Come, reap thy rich inheritance of love!
Bask in the fondness of a Mother's eye!
Nor wit nor eloquence her heart shall move
Like the first accents of thy feeble cry.

Haste, little captive, burst thy prison doors!
Launch on the living world, and spring to light!
Nature for thee displays her various stores,
Opens her thousand inlets of delight.

If charmed verse or muttered prayers had power,
With favouring spells to speed thee on thy way,
Anxious I'd bid my beads each passing hour,
Till thy wished smile thy mother's pangs o'erpay.

Ah! Why, Because the Dazzling Sun

EMILY BRONTË   1846

Ah! why, because the dazzling sun
Restored my earth to joy
Have you departed, every one,
And left a desert sky?

All through the night, your glorious eyes
Were gazing down in mine,
And with a full heart's thankful sighs
I blessed that watch divine!

I was at peace, and drank your beams
As they were life to me
And revelled in my changeful dreams
Like petrel on the sea.

Thought followed thought—star followed star
Through boundless regions on,
While one sweet influence, near and far,
Thrilled through and proved us one.

Why did the morning rise to break
So great, so pure a spell,
And scorch with fire the tranquil cheek
Where your cool radiance fell?

Blood-red he rose, and arrow-straight,
His fierce beams struck my brow;

The soul of Nature sprang elate,
But mine sank sad and low!

My lids closed down—yet through their veil
I saw him blazing still;
And bathe in gold the misty dale,
And flash upon the hill.

I turned me to the pillow then
To call back Night, and see
Your worlds of solemn light, again
Throb with my heart and me!

It would not do—the pillow glowed
And glowed both roof and floor,
And birds sang loudly in the wood,
And fresh winds shook the door.

The curtains waved, the wakened flies
Were murmuring round my room,
Imprisoned there, till I should rise
And give them leave to roam.

O Stars and Dreams and Gentle Night;
O Night and Stars return!
And hide me from the hostile light
That does not warm, but burn—

That drains the blood of suffering men;
Drinks tears, instead of dew:
Let me sleep through his blinding reign,
And only wake with you!

A Death blow is a Life blow to Some (816)

EMILY DICKINSON   1866

A Death blow is a Life blow to Some
Who till they died, did not alive become—
Who had they lived, had died but when
They died, Vitality begun.

The Mona Lisa Paragraph
from The Renaissance

WALTER PATER 1873

The presence that thus rose so strangely beside the waters, is expressive of what in the ways of a thousand years men had come to desire. Hers is the head upon which all "the ends of the world are come", and the eyelids are a little weary. It is a beauty wrought out from within upon the flesh, the deposit, little cell by cell, of strange thoughts and fantastic reveries and exquisite passions. Set it for a moment beside one of those white Greek goddesses or beautiful women of antiquity, and how would they be troubled by this beauty, into which the soul with all its maladies has passed! All the thoughts and experience of the world have been etched and moulded there, in that which they have of power to refine and make expressive the outward form, the animalism of Greece, the lust of Rome, the reverie of the middle age with its spiritual ambition and imaginative loves, the return of the Pagan world, the sins of the Borgias. She is older than the rocks among which she sits; like the vampire, she has been dead many times, and learned the secrets of the grave; and has been a diver in deep seas, and keeps their fallen day about her; and trafficked for strange webs with Eastern merchants: and, as Leda, was the mother of Helen of Troy, and, as Saint

Anne, the mother of Mary; and all this has been to her but as the sound of lyres and flutes, and lives only in the delicacy with which it has moulded the changing lineaments, and tinged the eyelids and the hands. The fancy of a perpetual life, sweeping together ten thousand experiences, is an old one; and modern thought has conceived the idea of humanity as wrought upon by, and summing up in itself, all modes of thought and life. Certainly Lady Lisa might stand as the embodiment of the old fancy, the symbol of the modern idea.

The Vampire

DELMIRA AGUSTINI 1910

Translated by Tim and Sofia Smith-Laing

In the sad lap of evening I called
upon your pain... To feel it was
to feel your heart beat out! You paled
right to your voice, two lids of wax

Came down... and silence too... You held
an ear to passing death... I who sank
your wound bit in my teeth — Could you feel?
Like biting at the hive's honeycomb sap.

Then I pressed again, traitor, sweetly,
on this heart of yours, wounded so deeply,
with the blade, exquisite, cruel and rare,
of an evil without name, till it sobbed red,
and my thousand mouths dipped their
thirst, cursed, to the fountain of your death.

Why was I your vampire of bitterness?
Am I a flower? Or a shoot born in darkness
of a species weaned on tears and ulcer flesh?

Oil and Blood

WILLIAM BUTLER YEATS 1928

In tombs of gold and lapis lazuli
Bodies of holy men and women exude
Miraculous oil, odour of violet.
But under heavy loads of trampled clay
Lie bodies of the vampires full of blood;
Their shrouds are bloody and their lips are wet.

I Am a Cowboy in the Boat of Ra

ISHMAEL REED   1972

> "The devil must be forced to reveal any such physical evil
> (potions, charms, fetishes, etc.) still outside the body
> and these must be burned." (Rituale Romanum, published
> 1947, endorsed by the coat-of-arms and introductory
> letter from Francis Cardinal Spellman)

I am a cowboy in the boat of Ra,
sidewinders in the saloons of fools
bit my forehead like O
the untrustworthiness of Egyptologists
who do not know their trips. Who was that
dog-faced man? they asked, the day I rode
from town.

School marms with halitosis cannot see
the Nefertiti fake chipped on the run by slick
germans, the hawk behind Sonny Rollins' head or
the ritual beard of his axe; a longhorn winding
its bells thru the Field of Reeds.

I am a cowboy in the boat of Ra. I bedded
down with Isis, Lady of the Boogaloo, dove
deep down in her horny, stuck up her Wells-Far-ago
in daring midday getaway. "Start grabbing the
blue," I said from top of my double crown.

I am a cowboy in the boat of Ra. Ezzard Charles
of the Chisholm Trail. Took up the bass but they
blew off my thumb. Alchemist in ringmanship but a
sucker for the right cross.

I am a cowboy in the boat of Ra. Vamoosed from
the temple i bide my time. The price on the wanted
poster was a-going down, outlaw alias copped my stance
and moody greenhorns were making me dance;
while my mouth's
shooting iron got its chambers jammed.

I am a cowboy in the boat of Ra. Boning-up in
the ol' West i bide my time. You should see
me pick off these tin cans whippersnappers. I
write the motown long plays for the comeback of
Osiris. Make them up when stars stare at sleeping
steer out here near the campfire. Women arrive
on the backs of goats and throw themselves on
my Bowie.

I am a cowboy in the boat of Ra. Lord of the lash,
the Loup Garou Kid. Half breed son of Pisces and
Aquarius. I hold the souls of men in my pot. I do
the dirty boogie with scorpions. I make the bulls
keep still and was the first swinger to grape the taste.

I am a cowboy in his boat. Pope Joan of the
Ptah Ra. C/mere a minute willya doll?
Be a good girl and
bring me my Buffalo horn of black powder
bring me my headdress of black feathers

bring me my bones of Ju-Ju snake
go get my eyelids of red paint.
Hand me my shadow

I'm going into town after Set

I am a cowboy in the boat of Ra

look out Set   here i come Set
to get Set   to sunset Set
to unseat Set to Set down Set

>   usurper of the Royal couch
>   imposter RAdio of Moses' bush
>   party pooper O hater of dance
>   vampire outlaw of the milky way

Pocket Vampire

DOROTHY BARRESI

I reconcile myself to need.
To wanting stinging, aptest,
seigneurial, pugnacious,
handsome as always cracking wise in my
blood things, I think—by pulp
supply of roots or tearing teeth, and/or ardor
for what I vow against but carry
always like my secret self,
the bitten bride,
to rat-consecrated, moon-wharf glum's
glee in gotten-up peignoir
dripping not daisies but rotten, long-aborning
lickable black roses, the smaller
the better to hide my privacy in: it's
pretty good getting, that bite I flirt
but never stick my neck out for.
Yes, Your Woundship.
Would a quibble count? Just one lick?
Damn me. Then,
back into the bidden, unblessed
dark with you, my tiny prince
of dirty comity.
Sin simulacrum.

Charles Baudelaire and I Meet in the Oval Garden

JOHN YAU   2022

Which windowpane are you beating your wings against
  today?
I am not as stubborn as you: I am flying straight into that
  delicious fire.

Buckets of bubbling tar and champagne await us at the *Blue
  Chalet*.
Do you skip like this because you have been invited into
  our hopping choir?

I am not as stubborn as you: I am flying straight into that
  delicious fire.
I thought you were going to the theater in your new
  cabriolet.

Do you skip like this because you have been invited into
  our hopping choir?
Yes, I do know the difference between a martini and a
  matinee.

I thought you were going to the theater in your new
  cabriolet.
They say that the latest strain hiding in the shadows is a
  yellow vampire.

Yes, I do know the difference between a martini and a matinee.
You have your subdivisions and high rises, while I have my dumpy shire.

They say that the latest strain hiding in the shadows is a yellow vampire.
Don't worry—my ancestors are sewn up in overcoats and on full display.

You have your subdivisions and high rises, while I have my dumpy shire.
When it comes to curry and gin, I say: "Let's wallow in Combray."

Don't worry—my ancestors are sewn up in overcoats and on full display.
Which windowpane are you beating your wings against today?

When it comes to curry and gin, I say: "Let's wallow in Combray"
Buckets of bubbling tar and champagne await us at the *Blue Chalet*.

ALSO AVAILABLE
FROM PUSHKIN PRESS

Sheridan Le Fanu
Carmilla

The Cult Classic that inspired Dracula

Pushkin Press

THE DAMNED THING

Weird & Ghostly Tales

AMBROSE BIERCE

"His greatness is in no danger of eclipse"
H.P. LOVECRAFT

pushkin press

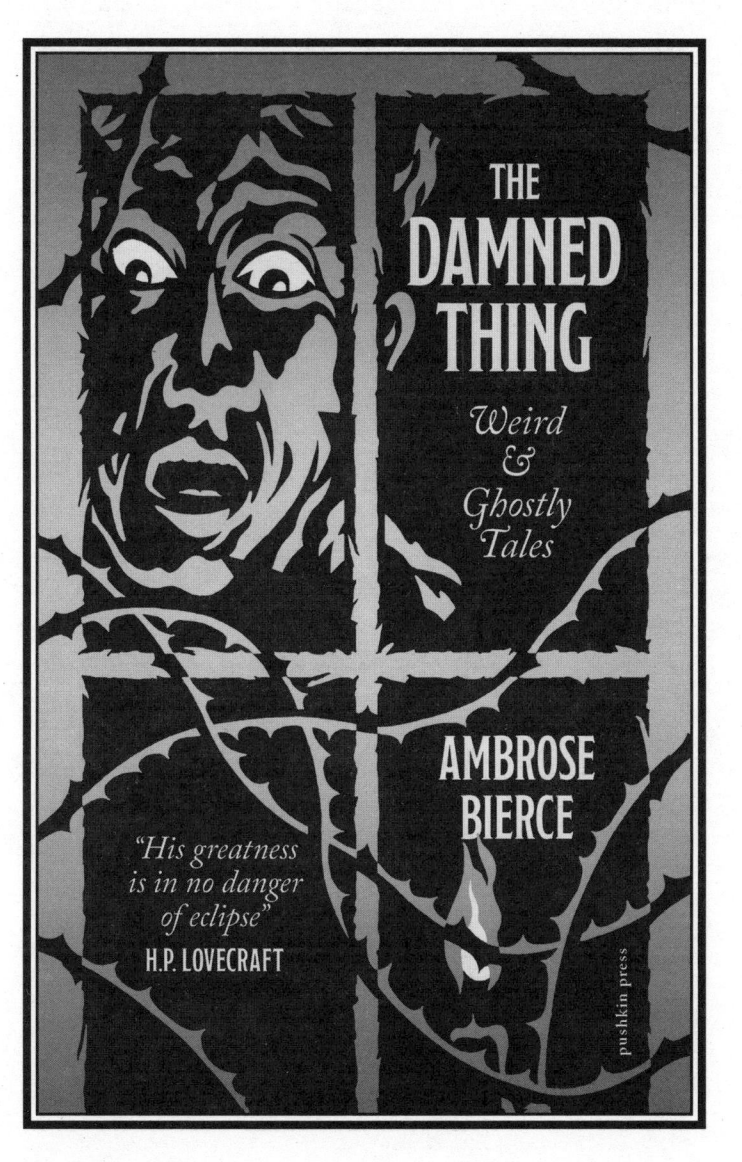

ANCIENT SORCERIES

PUSHKIN PRESS

'Of the quality of Mr. Blackwood's genius there can be no dispute'
H.P. LOVECRAFT

Algernon Blackwood

'One of the greatest weird tales ever written'
H.P. Lovecraft

THE KING IN YELLOW

ROBERT W. CHAMBERS

PUSHKIN PRESS